Recensere:

THE L⦿ST QUEEN

Morgan M. Steele

Other Works by Morgan M. Steele:

L.O.S.T. and F.O.U.N.D.

O Positive

Doing Just Fine

The Averagers: a parody

Map of Recensere created with Inkarnate.

Steele Bookcase Publishing

Cover art by Viergacht of Self Pub Book Covers

ISBN-10: 1732663017

ISBN-13: 978-1-7326630-1-5

For Uncle Steve.

Thank you for opening my eyes to the magical world around me.

Recensere

The Isle of Highland

The Wynter

The Elven Lands

The Borderlands

Faerfolk Glade

Marshwood Clearing

River's End

The Stillgreen Forests

The Frynge

MORGAN M. STEELE

PROLOGUE

The year was 1984. Three teenagers walked through the woods, their boots crunching in the fresh autumn leaves. So far, their search had been unsuccessful, but with any luck, that was about to change.

The map in Johnny's hand said that the ruins were right off of the path, just a little ways further. For Selena's sake, he hoped so; she didn't look so good. Delphinus was carrying her. Johnny told them that he should have stayed home with her, but Selena had insisted on coming—on being here when they found it.

Now, he wasn't so sure he had made the right choice, letting her come. Hopefully, the book would have all the answers they needed. Johnny shined the flashlight on a sign just off of the dirt road they had been following. "Hang in there."

It was old and wooden, painted over a thousand times, but he could still make out the indents of the ancient symbols. When he traced them with his fingertip, he felt something wash over him...something he couldn't describe, but it made the mark on his collarbone burn.

They were headed the right way.

"I feel it too," Selena whispered. She curled further into Delphinus's chest, trying to sink into his warmth. Her breath curled up in puffs of steam, rising into the starry night sky.

A quarter mile more and they were there, a broken piece of a castle tower, submerged partially in the ground. A single remnant of a once great fortress. The only thing that survived the Shift.

Delphinus looked around the forest and found a spot in the leaves where he could lean Selena against a tree.

She sensed his intentions and shook her head. "I can stand."

Delphinus set her on her feet, but kept a wary arm around her. Johnny had his flashlight held between his teeth while he

3

tried to pry the door open. No such luck. Delphinus motioned Johnny over and shifted Selena from himself to the taller brunette. Then, he raised his hand.

A ball of light began to manifest, growing until it launched from Delphinus' palm and blasted the decrepit wooden door from its hinges. The display was a little much for Johnny's liking, or his eyes for that matter, but the job was done. Now they could get in.

Johnny adjusted his grip on Selena and helped her stumble through the door of the haphazard stone structure. It had been the Starcastle. The once-great home of the few Starchildren that managed to escape the Collapse. There had been so many, but now, the gene was buried deep, only unearthed every few generations.

Selena was one of them. At the moment, she was the only one left.

Something was happening in Beacon Point, an awakening of sorts. With any luck, this remnant of a lost world would bring them the answers they needed to prevent another supernatural extinction.

Johnny helped Selena kneel in front of the wooden chest that was too untouched by the years gone by and the overall destruction around it to be anything but enchanted. There was no way it wasn't protected by some sort of —

"Magic," he murmured. He kept an arm around Selena as she looked down at the relic.

It was fine, polished wood, intricately carved. The lock didn't look like anything either of the three teens recognized, although Delphinus swore it looked familiar. Somewhere in his fried memories, there was something like this from a time when he was a little less...human.

Hints of a memory tugged at him. Little blips on the radar. The Hevynrealm was all a distant dream, but he knew it had happened. And he knew that somehow, at some time in his existence, he had been here at Starcastle before it had all been blown to hell. In fact, he was pretty sure he had been the one that locked the chest in front of them. But he didn't have the key; Selena did.

She was a protector, a guardian, a vessel of immeasurable power, and Johnny and Delphinus both knew that when it came down to it, she would save them all.

Selena reached forward and pressed her hand against the lock. She felt the carvings, the ancient fingerprints, and she could feel the magic wrapped around it, thrumming in beat with her own. With a click, it opened.

Johnny pulled the lock off of the chest and helped Delphinus lift its heavy wooden lid. The wave of star Magyk that emerged had enough force to knock both boys off their feet. Selena, however, was unaffected, the surge only causing her white hair to glow for a few moments before dimming back to its usual platinum blonde. Johnny and Delphinus scrambled to their knees beside Selena on the cracked stone floors of what used to be a tower.

Selena moved closer, leaning against the wood. Pale light shined from her fist, illuminating the contents of the giant wooden box. There were stray chess pieces, a bag of marbles, a child's doll. And at the very bottom of the chest, hiding under all of it, was a large brown leather book with ornate scripted golden symbols.

Johnny looked to Delphinus and Selena for a reaction. He, unlike the other two, was very much and had always been human. He didn't know much about the Other World Delphinus told Selena about. Sure, Selena had never been there either, but she was a Starchild, not a Mortal. Johnny wanted to help her, he really did, he just wasn't sure how.

5

Selena picked up the book with shaking hands, skimming over the letters on the cover with a careful finger. The words seemed to glow at her touch. The ancient symbols rearranged, shifting, moving, floating around until they settled.

"What is it?" Johnny asked. His Mortal eyes couldn't see anything aside from the strange runes. Only Selena could read it. Delphinus looked to the white-haired girl, his heart racing in anticipation.

"The Legend of Recensere."

Chapter 1

THERE WAS A GIRL

Arya Miller had grown up all her life in the village of River's End. From her backyard, she could see the spot where the path left the village and touched the Veil, a place she knew she could never go, but she never wanted to. Arya lived a very normal life and she liked it that way.

She liked her chores at the mill and tending to her mother's garden. She liked to walk through the village's makeshift market at the heart of town. She liked her friends and her family and her cozy little house next to the blacksmith's workshop. Most of all, she liked her friend Henry Smith.

Henry wasn't like Arya, and maybe that was why she admired him so much. Arya was a homebody. She liked to stay in the village and tend to their cow and sew her skirts, but Henry wanted more and always had since they were very young. He spent his days dreaming about what there might be out beyond the Veil or even just outside River's End. Henry's father wanted him to take up the mantle of the village's blacksmith when he retired, but Henry knew that the day he turned eighteen, he was going off to find his place.

That scared Arya like nothing else.

The village was safe. The village was home. That was what her father had always told her; anything beyond the Veil was dangerous and Magykal and unforgiving. If she wandered beyond the borders of her town, she'd surely be snatched up and killed by whatever forces roamed out there, lurking in the shadows. So, every night, Arya made sure her window was shut tight and lit a candle to keep out the dark things that might come for her.

But it was too nice of a day to be concerned with such things.

7

Arya handed the baker a few coins in exchange for a little loaf of bread to go along with her jam. Henry had asked her to meet him at the hill so they could watch the sunset on the Veil. They did this sometimes when Henry was troubled. It helped him clear his muddled mind to talk to her.

So, just as the market stalls were closing, Arya ran off down the path to the edge of the village, and then up the hill where Henry was sitting on a brown woven blanket.

Everything in the village was brown. Arya had only noticed this a few years before while she was hanging some of her brown dresses up to dry. Everyone in the River's End was Mortal, and therefore, they had brown hair and brown eyes. When the Rebellion had happened, just before Arya was born, as her mother had told her, all of the color had been cut out of their lives. Their houses were brown. Their paths were brown. Their clothes were brown. The grass grew brown, and the trees of the village seemed to be trapped in an eternal autumn, their leaves never changing a shade until they fell out and the icy winters swept in from the north. But when they grew back in, their leaves only buds, they grew in brown. It was boring, but it was the way things were. She had never known anything else.

This was the only place in the whole village that they could get a glimpse at color. The sunset would send the sky into a frenzy of warmth, red and orange and pink. During the day, clouds blotted out the skies Arya had been told were once blue, but at dusk, the spell over the sky broke for a short period of time and allowed them to see these vivid hues.

"Amazing, isn't it?" The lights flickered across Henry's smooth skin and he picked at the grass. "I heard out there it's like this all the time."

"I bet."

"Sure beats clouds."

Arya only hummed in response, taking a seat next to her best friend in the entire world. They would have to agree to disagree. Though blue cloudless skies did indeed sound beautiful, Arya heard from her parents that back in the times before the gray blotted out the sun, they had gotten angry red burns on their skin from the vengeful ball of light.

Henry smiled at her. He liked the way the light made her hair almost look red. He knew that there were some Magykfolk with red hair. The idea was amusing, he supposed. Intriguing even. People who had hair colors other than brown. Maybe somewhere in that Magykal land, there were people with hair every color of the rainbow, another thing he'd only heard about in stories.

"Did you bring the jam?"

"I did." She handed him the small glass jar and he twisted the lid off. They each tore a small piece of bread off of the loaf and dipped it into the jar. The jam was sweet, thick, the only thing that tasted good in the entire village as far as Henry was concerned. Though, for someone on a diet of almost entirely potato stew, variation of any kind was more than welcome.

"And I got *you* something." Henry reached into his satchel and pulled out a small treasure, hiding it in his large hands.

Arya's eyebrow ticked upward. It wasn't often that Henry brought her surprises. "Did you, now?"

Henry pulled away his long fingers to reveal a fine white stone set into a brooch. It dangled from a golden chain, and the way it felt...there was no way it was from River's End. The amulet had an energy she couldn't describe. Something otherworldly. Something that must have come...

She looked over at the glassy Veil, its protective border drifting in a bubble around the rich forests teeming with Magyk.

"How...*where*...?" Arya knew how much the land beyond the Veil meant to Henry. Him giving her something from that place meant a whole lot in her book. It was rare that anything escaped the enchanted barrier, rarer yet that it was something beautiful like this rather than an outbreak of wild fungus or hordes of flying stinging things.

"I found it. On the bridge." Henry pointed to the place the path crossed the river, where a crude stone bridge stood. "It felt like it was meant for you, so I used some of my father's tools to clean it off, fix up the chain..." Henry rubbed over the iridescent gem with his thumb before pressing the gift into his best friend's hand. "I actually had a question for you."

She grinned coyly. "Perhaps I have an answer."

Henry looked out towards the Veil, and Arya's heart sank. She knew where this conversation was headed.

"I was wondering if you would come with me to seek out the Three-Eyed Frynge Wytch. Maybe she has a way to get through the Veil."

"Henry...I don't think that's a good idea." The girl spoke softly, in an attempt to spare his heart from breaking. "The Magyklands are dangerous. And Frynge Wytches...they only ever want trouble."

"There has to be a way to get in. There *has* to be...this can't be it." He sighed, laying back on the grass and staring up at the pink-tickled sky. "I can't spend the rest of my life in this boring village making swords until I'm old and wrinkled."

"What else would you do? What even *is* there beyond the Veil for people like us?"

"I don't know. I'd find somewhere I could live in there. There has to be somewhere."

"A place in there where they don't hate Mortals? Good luck with that."

"I just need to see it. Just once." He closed his eyes and exhaled a long breath, letting the dreams drift away on the breeze.

There was something else he'd invited her there to talk about. "I have another question, if it's not too much to ask."

"Yes?"

"Arya, how long have we known each other?" He took her hand in his own.

She giggled. "Only our whole lives. Sorry, I haven't exactly been counting the days."

"Precisely. Our houses have been side by side forever. I can't think of a single day I haven't seen you in some capacity." Henry chuckled at his racing heart and shook his head. He'd known Arya all this time, and yet he was still nervous? Silly. "What I'm saying is…we're both getting to that age where our parents, if we don't do something about it, will marry us off."

"And?"

"Well, you're the miller's daughter. I'm the blacksmith's son. If we're being honest, the only girl in this village I want to spend the rest of my days with is you. So, if you'd have me, some-day…"

Arya's eyes widened, and then, in a moment that made Henry's heart race and eyebrows furrow, they turned blue.

"If my parents tried to marry me to anyone else, I think I'd die." Arya laughed, unaware of the problem Henry's very brown Mortal eyes were fixed on. "Do I have something on my face? What's wrong?" Arya wiped the corner of her lips in hopes of finding a stray bit of jam.

"Y-your eyes. Arya, they're — " Henry grabbed her wrist and ran down the hill to the river. The current there was slow enough for the girl to make out her reflection. And indeed, he was right: her eyes were blue, not brown like everyone else in the village, like they had been for her entire life. No, they were blue. Blue like a Fae.

"Oh my gods."

"What do we do?" Henry asked, a bewildered look on his face.

"I don't know." She shook her head. It was then that the teens heard the voice echoing over the hills.

"Arya! Dinner!" It was her mother's voice. Oh, Katherine Miller. She was a doting and loving mother, but she was indeed *doting*. Arya could barely leave her mother's sight without the woman going crazy. The only time she could catch a break was when she went to the market or spent time with Henry.

"Coming, Mother!" she shouted in reply. She looked to Henry for a plan. The clever boy *always* had a plan.

"Pretend you haven't noticed." He whispered to her very intensely. The blacksmith's son took her hands in his and wrapped them tightly around the necklace. "And for the love of the gods, don't let them see this."

At this point, Henry was fairly certain the necklace was the cause of her sudden change, and he wasn't all that far off. The necklace had triggered something in Arya that she didn't know was there, but she would learn of it soon enough.

Chapter 2

THE SECRETS THEY KEPT

All throughout dinner, Arya tried her best to be oblivious, but she couldn't ignore the looks her parents were exchanging. John and Katherine Miller had always been cautious not to let Arya go too near the Veil for fear of what she might find. All these years, they had been successful, but now that her eighteenth birthday was rapidly approaching, they would have to work faster.

The people of River's End kept a secret. One that was only spoken of in the tunnels that connected their houses beneath the village. Arya Miller was not an ordinary girl, nor had she ever been. A Wytch's Magyk had been keeping the girl's true nature at bay all these years. Unfortunately for them, this Wytch had died only a year ago and the Magyk had run dry.

So, the Mortals of River's End, desperate to keep their darkest secret, had pulled together the beginnings of a hasty scheme. If a Wytch couldn't give them Magyk to keep the girl Mortal, they'd have to make some themselves.

Of course, the key to making any good potion is testing it, and it wasn't like the Mortals could test it on themselves. After all, they were already Mortal. If they used the potion on themselves, it wouldn't have any effect at all.

Instead, the Mortals turned to kidnapping the little Magykfolk that wandered out of the Veil. Namely, the greedy little Leprechauns that had been stealing their shiny treasures for years. Most of the tiny fiery-haired creatures had caught on to the Mortals' dangerous game and had stopped coming to River's End for fear of being kidnapped and used in their mad experiments. But Finnigan Ó Floinn had not been informed of the situation.

Finnigan was indeed a greedy little thing. Like the rest of his kind, he could never resist a shiny trinket. So, when he heard about all of the little treasures in River's End, he couldn't help but take a peek in the blacksmith's house. That was when James Smith found him trying to smuggle out all of his fresh jeweled rings.

The blacksmith scooped up the little red-haired leprechaun in his large calloused hands with a wicked grin on his face. Finally, after several weeks without one, they had another test subject.

Finnigan squirmed and struggled, trying to get free, but no matter how quick or small he was, he couldn't slip through the man's fingers. And then, James locked him in a little wooden box until the town meeting that night.

Once dark had fallen over River's End and all of the young ones had gone to bed, the adults of the village convened in the tunnels beneath the town. When James turned the box over to John, the man gave it a little shake to hear their precious cargo rustle around inside it. This was just what they needed. With any luck, they could brew the potion tonight, test it tomorrow, and have it in Arya's oatmeal before she ever noticed anything had changed.

"Ye'll never get away with this! Ye hear? Ye big beasties!" The little box shook with the Leprechaun's protests. They set his wooden prison on a shelf adjacent to their makeshift alchemy station and weighed it down with a thick leather book.

"That's what they all say." John gave the box a harsh flick and then walked through the passage back to his house. His steps were careful, as to not disturb the old beams that made up the floor. A peek through the door of Arya's bedroom told him that she was in bed, sound asleep. So, feeling much better about the day to come, he left and went to his own bed where Katherine was waiting for him.

As soon as Arya heard his footsteps traveling further down the hall, she cracked an eye open and saw that her father's shadow had left the doorframe. She didn't hear any creaks in the floorboards or any voices in the room next door. So, she waited a few more minutes and then slid her feet out from under her blanket. Arya crept to the window, her bare soles soft against the wooden floor, and carefully pulled apart the beige curtains.

On the path in front of her house, approaching the fence that stood around the yard beneath her bedroom, she could make out a flickering candle and the frame of a boy she knew all too well. Henry motioned her forward. Arya slung a satchel over her shoulder, tucked her brown leather boots under her arm, and carefully scaled down the autumn vines that clung to the side of her house.

"I have a plan." Henry whispered once she was standing at the fence. His breath caught when he noticed how her skin seemed to sparkle in the candlelight. "Tomorrow, during the Harvest Festival, we need to make an appearance and then disappear. I found something in the house…something you need to see. But we have to be quiet. I overheard Maryanne Woods talking to my mother. Something is happening tomorrow night. Once you see it, you'll finally believe me that this place isn't as safe as you thought it was."

"I *do* believe you." Arya rested her hand on the top of the fence and it was soon covered by Henry's larger, warmer one. "My parents didn't say a word about my eyes and then Papa disappeared after dinner and didn't come back until bed."

"So did my father."

"Something is going on here." Arya looked into Henry's very Mortal eyes as he gazed into her blue, Magyk-filled ones.

15

Something kind and comforting lingered there, setting her at ease even in times like these.

He smiled softly, in a way that always gave Arya hope. "And we're going to get to the bottom of it."

The next day came and went fairly quickly. Arya busied herself with helping the other villagers prepare for the Harvest Festival, pretending not to notice their subtle looks of shock when they got a glimpse of her up close. The adults were the same, for the most part, staring at her a bit, but normal otherwise. It was the kids and the villagers around her age that were the most curious, although most of them were too polite to actually say anything about her odd eyes. There was one particularly young child that had asked her if it was contagious, only to have his mother shush him and scold him for being rude.

Something was being hidden from them, that much was obvious. They only hoped that by the end of the night, they would figure out what.

Once the sun began to set, Katherine called Arya inside to help her daughter prepare for the festival. Harvest was the only time the people of River's End had a celebration. Some of them quietly honored Rebellion Day in remembrance of those who were lost in the war against the Magykfolk. In the spring times before the Rebellion, there used to be a Festival of Flowers, but since the Mortals had all been banished to the Borderlands, they didn't have any flowers to celebrate, not except for the flowering weeds that rooted themselves in their gardens and suffocated their crops, a gift from the High Healer of the Faeries who still mourned the loss of her eldest daughter to the war the Mortals had started.

Katherine reached into the chest at the end of the bed she and John slept in. In it, she had stashed away something she had been waiting to share with her daughter for as long as the girl had been in their lives. It was a wreath made from Recensere's autumn leaves. She had gotten it from one of her friends, a Fae, back before the Rebellion, when she was only a girl about Arya's age. It was enchanted to never lose its rich red autumn hues. A vivid splash of color in a sea of brown.

This crown of the harvest times was indeed a beautiful gift, but it served a purpose. Arya knew from the moment her mother laid the ring in her fresh curls that this was meant to make her stand out so the others could watch the girl with the blue eyes. But living in a village full of people who all had brown hair and brown eyes gave Arya a distinct advantage. She could pass off the crown to any of the other girls and the people who were trying to watch her would be none the wiser. Well, at least until they got a good look at her face.

Once she was wearing the nicest brown dress she owned, Arya made her way to the center of town. It was one of the only times the whole village came together like this, everyone in one place. Children chased each other through the streets, laughing. Groups of girls were making crowns from whatever vines they could find. A handful of musicians played their poorly-tuned instruments, creating a chaotic harmony for the people to dance to. Finally, after searching for him for a long few moments, she spotted Henry leaning against the fence surrounding the maypole.

"Nice...wreath."

"Enchanted to always be orange. Coincidence?"

"Not likely." Henry scratched the thin layer of scruff that had settled on his chin and jaw. "They're keeping an eye on you. Notice how the mirrors disappeared this morning?"

Now that he mentioned it, Arya realized he was right. There wasn't a single time that day that she had seen her own reflection. The Mortals were a lot of things, but they weren't dumb. "Yeah, I thought that was odd."

"So, who are you going to ditch it on?" He surveyed their options, weighing the consequences of each.

"I was thinking Margaret. Nice girl. Oblivious. The perfect target."

"Agreed." Henry glanced over at the girl in question. She was indeed pretty, and twice as oblivious as she was kind. Additionally, she looked enough like Arya that their plan might just work. "Alright, give it here. I'll take care of it. Go hide in the shadows behind my house. I'll be there in a few minutes."

"Thank you." Arya took the crown off of her head and handed it to Henry.

He walked off through the crowd of people wrapping varying shades of brown ribbons around the tall hunk of wood that had once been a tree. Arya looked both ways, searching the crowd to make sure all of the watching eyes were no longer on her for the first time in the past day.

Invisible once again, the blue-eyed girl slipped into the shadows behind the Smith house. The flames from the smelter out back were no more than tiny flickers, the only light in the house a lonely candle in the window. Arya waited there for a few minutes, crystal blue irises scanning the faces in the crowd for any sign of her father before she finally heard the sound of Henry's boots crunching in the dry brown grass.

"Margaret is clueless as always. I think she's enjoying the newfound attention, but I'm not sure how much time it'll buy us."

"Did you see my father out there? Or your father?"

Henry thought about it and then glanced back at the Festival briefly before turning around to face her again. "No. I didn't."

"That's what I'm worried about."

Henry looked to Arya with a mix of concern, knowingness, and dread. "Don't worry. I think I know where they are."

Chapter 3

UNDER RIVER'S END

Henry took Arya's hand and led her through his dark house. She had been inside it many times, but it felt different now that she knew something was amiss. The only person in the entire village that she could trust anymore had interlocked his fingers with hers.

Because this was the blacksmith's house, evidence of James' craft was displayed everywhere. Intricate shields were mounted on the wall, his finest swords hanging from hooks as though they were as mundane as a cloak or cap. Spare daggers littered otherwise empty surfaces, and attached to the wall in the front room, there was a large cabinet filled with the nicer jewelry he had made over the years.

Henry spent a lot of his time here. Arya had known that already, as he didn't show any interest in going into smithing like his father. Tucked away in his room, through his slightly opened door, she could see scrolls and scrolls of the maps he had drawn up based on the stories of the adults that had actually gotten to live in the Magyklands. Henry had shown his collection to Arya once, and she was impressed with the details he'd gathered. Some of them were a bit skewed, as some of the village elders' memories weren't as sharp as they had been once, but for the most part, the estimates he'd made about the locations of landmarks and territories seemed to match up without too much contradiction.

As they walked further through the dark room, it became evident that Henry knew just where to step on the floor so the wood wouldn't creak under his feet and he helped Arya through the motions until they were standing in front of Mrs. Smith's bookshelf. He scanned the titles written on the brown leather spines, his fingertip tracing their smooth edges until he found the title he was searching for.

A History of Magykfolk.

When Henry pulled the book from the shelf, it didn't come loose. Instead, the wooden structure creaked open to reveal a secret tunnel dug into the ground under the village. A few stray lanterns hung on the wall of the dirt cavern. Henry took one of them from its hook and held Arya's hand with the other, helping her down the steep passage. When they finally made it to the place where the tunnels joined, Arya was sure the space must have covered the entire area beneath the town. She was certain this had taken years or decades to build. It was complex and well crafted, and from what she could see from the end of the tunnel she and Henry had come from, it was well stocked with enough supplies to start a war.

Henry grabbed Arya and pulled her into a smaller side tunnel, one that looked hastily made. In the wall, there was a tiny little hole the size of a fist that provided a glimpse into the rest of the room. Sure enough, John Miller and James Smith were both present along with some of the other villagers that had disappeared from the Harvest Festival celebrations.

They were standing over a wooden chair in a small semicircle. John was holding a vial of a glowing substance. It was a color Arya didn't recognize. Warmer than blue but not quite pink. It shimmered in a way that could only be Magyk, like how the sunset gleamed off of the river on the hill, but this shimmering held a darker feeling, something much more sinister.

James had taken a little wooden box off of a shelf. It shook, holding something Arya doubted would set her at ease that all of this was a big mistake and the people of the village were just pulling a joke on her. She couldn't shake the feeling of dread that settled deep in her stomach. It wasn't a coincidence that all of these strange things were happening at once…

John reached into the box and pulled out a struggling little creature. Arya's heart raced. She had never seen a Magykfolk in person before. He had fiery red hair that rivaled the shade of orange the leaves around her head had been. His clothes were green, as she heard the grass and leaves used to be once before the Rebellion when all of the Mortals were exiled to this drab place.

The little creature couldn't be more than a few inches tall, maybe five at most. He struggled against the large hand holding him, but he couldn't break from the miller's strong grip. John dripped a few drops of the potion into the leprechaun's little mouth, and though he tried to resist, he couldn't stop the flow of liquid into his tiny body. Just a few drops were enough to trigger a change.

John set him in the wooden chair sitting in the center of the dirt chamber. Arya squinted to see what was happening. As the creature was so small, it was hard to make out exactly what he was doing, but it seemed his little head began to droop, drowsiness conquering his tiny body.

Arya's eyebrows furrowed and something clicked in her frazzled mind. She recognized the symptom almost immediately. The very same thing had happened to her on a few cloudy mornings. She'd be eating her oatmeal, sitting at the table like any other day, and then the strangest fit of exhaustion would take over and she'd feel numb, fuzzy, unable to form a coherent thought for a few moments until it faded, leaving her feeling an odd sense of normalcy.

Next, the leprechaun's arms and legs began to stretch and grow, elongating and widening into Mortal-sized limbs. He scrunched up his face and groaned in pain as his muscles and bones and everything else shifted and grew into place. He felt bigger. Too big. Too tall. Suddenly the room around him felt smaller. The chair was no longer a spacious surface big enough to hold half of the people from his village, and was instead almost too small for his new form.

The giants before him were no longer giants at all. They were his size now.

Finnigan was still too drowsy to notice or care about the absence of his Magyk as it rushed out of him in a frenzy of sparkling steam, leaving his fiery red hair a dull shade of brown and his vivid green eyes no different than John's or James'.

The blacksmith and miller coughed and waved it away, fanning at the mist that smelled of wet grass and mud. They took stock of the boy sitting in front of them. Now that he was finally large enough to see clearly, John noticed that he didn't look any older than Arya, freckles dotting just about every inch of his skin, which was tanned from his days frolicking in the bright Recenserean sunshine. It made him sick with jealousy to remember how beautiful the world inside the Veil was, that wonderful world the Mortals were banished from.

John watched as the drowsiness slowly left the Leprechaun's body.

Finnigan sat up, his fingers trembling as he looked over the new Mortal form he was trapped in. His heart raced, and he studied his hands, his legs, his chest. His lungs heaved with heavy breaths. He forced himself out of the chair, ready to fight the Mortals that had done this to him, that had changed him and made him like them: gross, hideous, and worst of all, boring.

"What have ye done to me?" He took a quick step forward and raised his fist. His movements were slower now, he noticed bitterly. They'd stolen his Magyk and the skip in his step with it. "Change me back!"

"I'm afraid you won't be yourself for quite some time, you little Magyk freak." James spat at him.

John gave the boy a shove and then James subdued him, taking advantage of his clumsy, awkward state. The other villagers that had assembled helped tie up the Magykfolk and bind him to the chair. Then, once their work was done, they started to head up through the various tunnels that connected their houses to this secret laboratory of sorts, John lingering long enough to hear Finnigan's final call.

"Yer just leaving me here?" Finnigan struggled against the ropes, but to no avail. The potion had wiped him out, exhausting him more than any thieving adventure ever had. His limbs felt so heavy. How did Mortals do this, living without Magyk? It was the worst. His Leprechaun liveliness had been completely vaporized along with his speed and prowess, leaving him a sluggish Mortal.

"You can shout all you want, but no one will hear you over the Festival music." John told him with a wicked grin.

Arya didn't like the look on her father's face, the way his thick eyebrows framed the malicious look in his eyes, or how mean his smile looked with half of his face concealed in shadow. He looked like a different person, unrecognizable. In all her years living under his roof, all the years he had raised her, she had never seen a look that had scared her as much as that one did. Even when he'd been angry with her when she misbehaved, he'd never been *mean*. It was a side of him she never knew existed, and she wished she never had to.

If the Mortals of the village had their way, Arya would be the next to end up like the unfortunate Leprechaun, and her eyes would be back to brown, as they had always been. She wouldn't be different anymore.

She...wouldn't be different anymore.

"Arya, you okay?" Henry whispered, careful not to let the former Leprechaun hear him just yet.

"I'm fine." Arya replied with what was obviously a lie. She was not okay. Not after witnessing something like that.

"Let's get him out of here."

"Okay," she agreed.

Henry stepped out of the little passage hidden in the wall first and Arya followed slowly, trying not to startle the Leprechaun.

Finnigan was still crying for help in the center of the room, his voice only a weak call. Even if no one could hear him, he had to try.

"Are you okay?" Arya asked him softly. It took Finnigan a few seconds to register that someone had talked to him. He blinked a few times and looked up at the stranger. In a world full of brown-eyed Mortals, this one had blue eyes. So, not a Mortal, technically. Suddenly, he was very embarrassed to be in his current state. "My name is—"

"D-don't look at me!" Finnigan turned his face away from her. "I'm hideous."

"You're *Mortal*." Henry shook his head and set to work on the bonds that were holding the boy hostage.

"Exactly. That's my point." Finnigan looked down at himself, the reality of the situation still not quite real to him. He couldn't be Mortal. It was impossible. It was *horrible*.

"Do you feel alright?" Arya asked softly. There was kindness in her blue eyes, Finnigan decided. "Does anything hurt?"

"*Everything* hurts." He groaned. Soreness had bloomed and blossomed in every single one of his limbs, and he was sure that the bonds holding him weren't helping any.

Finally, Henry got the ropes loose using the dagger attached to his belt. If he had learned anything from his father, it was that a good blacksmith never went anywhere without one.

"Can you stand?" she asked.

Finnigan nodded and then tried to get to his feet, but his legs weren't cooperating. They shook like a dog during a thunderstorm, and then he collapsed back onto the chair. That wasn't going to work. "No, I cannot."

25

"Let me help you." Henry and Arya each offered a hand and helped him up. They both realized very quickly that the Leprechaun that had once been around five inches tall was now easily half a foot taller than each of them. Arya, standing a little shorter than the average Mortal girl, felt tiny standing beside him, and even Henry at his slightly taller height was put on edge a little bit.

"I think I'm going to be sick." Finnigan's head spun at the height difference. This was not okay. He was not okay.

"It's fine. You're going to be fine," Arya reassured him, slinging one of his arms around her shoulders, an invitation for him to lean more of his weight against her, which he did. "We don't have much time."

"Arya and I can get you to the Veil. The Festival should keep the village folk busy." Henry thought on it for a few seconds. There was a chance, though slim, that someone would come to check on the former prisoner. If they were smart, they would have watched the Leprechaun in shifts, but he sensed that once they'd tested their potion on him, they didn't have much use for him. Henry didn't want to know what happened to the test subjects they were finished with...

"Busy enough, anyway." The almost-Mortal girl was concerned with something else altogether: if the Mortals of the village were all watching the Festival like hawks, how were they supposed to sneak this very tall person past them?

In the time they'd been standing there, Henry had been surveying their surroundings. More specifically, he'd been trying to determine which of the dozens of passages to use.

"Henry?" Arya looked to him for guidance. Until that day, Arya hadn't known there was a tunnel system beneath their village at all, so she certainly didn't have any idea where they should be headed.

"That one." He pointed across the bunker. "If my suspicions are correct, that tunnel should take us to the Hunters' house. We'd be close enough to the edge of town to sneak off to the Veil before anyone even knew we were gone."

Arya nodded. She trusted her clever friend. He was the only person she *could* trust anymore.

They walked across the room and up through the Hunters' tunnel, into their house, and out the back door. There weren't any lights there, so no one would notice them in the shadows. Next, they fled down the path, across the bridge, and right up to the edge of the woods, where the large shining bubble of the Veil was cast.

Arya looked at it in awe. Of course, she had seen it from afar many times, but never this close. A familiar tug pulled inside her chest. The Veil had terrified her for as long as she could remember. Her fathers' stories rang in her head, tales of Magykal monsters that snatched little girls in the night. She'd never wanted anything to do with the Magyklands and all of the creatures that lived within them, but the longer she thought about it and her parents and everything that had turned her away from the world within the Veil, the more her feelings turned sour. If her parents had told her all of those things, how much of it could *really* be true?

Up close like this, she could almost reach out and touch it, but then Henry brushed against the iridescent border and was knocked over from the force of the rebound Magyk.

No Mortals allowed. She had almost forgotten. Just like that, her hope fell. There had to be something wrong with this world for it to keep out the one person who wanted to be there the most. She could see on Henry's face that he was very visibly upset.

"Well, here you are," Henry said somewhat bitterly, motioning to the force that was put in place to bar people like him from the world he dreamed of exploring. Growing up in River's End, he'd always known that the Veil would throw him back just like any other Mortal. Yet as he stood in front of it with the stranger from beyond the wall and his best friend in the entire world, he realized something:

It wouldn't reject Arya.

Arya wasn't Mortal; that much he knew. She could have the adventure he had always dreamed of. Would he be jealous? Maybe a little, but was he certain beyond a shadow of a doubt she belonged *somewhere* in there? Yes. He was.

"Well, this is it. Do you think you'll be alright in there?" Arya asked Finnigan. At the sound of their voices, Henry wrenched himself from his thoughts.

"I think so, yes." Finnigan nodded. "Thank ye. Yer not so bad...for a couple of Mortals."

"Don't mention it. It's our parents' fault you're like this in the first place." Henry offered an apologetic smile.

Finnigan looked to each of his rescuers and then tentatively reached out to touch the magical force he called home. His fingers touched the Veil, going beyond and inside without the tiniest of a jolt. The potion had gotten rid of most of his Magyk, but apparently it hadn't gotten rid of all of it just yet. He stepped inside the boundaries unscathed.

"Hey, you, wait for a second, okay?" Henry asked Finnigan.

The boy nodded and took a few tentative steps further, finding a new balance in his strange Mortal body. It was then that Henry turned to Arya.

"Arya, listen. I know you love the village. I know it's your home and you've lived here forever and you want nothing more than to sit in your house and sew your skirts and get married off someday. But I don't want that for you. You could have so much more."

"Henry..."

"No, don't 'Henry' me. I don't get a choice, but you *do*. If I could choose, you know I'd go with you, but I can't. And it kills me to say this, but Arya, I don't think you've ever been Mortal. In all the years that I've known you, nothing has ever struck me about you as normal, as much as you've thought you are."

"But—"

"*Listen.*" He grabbed her shoulders and looked into her blue eyes that were now beginning to look more of a seafoam green color. The faint music from the Festival and stray cricket chirps filled the silence between them. Henry spoke like he was trying to instill her soul with fire. "Go with him. Find where you belong because it's obviously not around here, judging by your eyes."

"I can't just leave you here," she told him. Arya felt sick just thinking about it, but what choice did she have? If she went back to the village with Henry, her eyes would go back to being brown, and she'd never know why they were ever different in the first place. The Mortals were hiding something from her, and she wasn't going to find out what by sitting around and waiting for them to tell her. Finnigan was her only chance. She had to go with him. She *had* to. But that didn't mean she wanted to leave Henry behind. "I can't just leave you here pretending to be happy."

"I'll be happy knowing you're happy." Henry forced a smile for her sake, but it became more genuine the longer he looked at her. He couldn't be upset with Arya. He was *never* upset with Arya. She was the only person in all of River's End that listened to him even if she didn't understand, the only one that made him feel like maybe his crazy adventurous plans made sense somehow.

"I'm going to come back for you," she decided. "Once I figure out who—*what*—I really am, I'm coming back and I'm going to take you on the greatest adventure you've ever had."

"Is that a promise?"

"You can count on it." She spoke softly, trying to hide the tears that were bound to slip out of her eyes any second. They both knew they didn't have much time to dawdle.

Henry pulled Arya into his arms, kissed the top of her head as he had so many times before, and then grabbed the necklace from the pouch on her dress and fastened the clasp around the girl's neck. He knew this was meant to happen. That no matter what the universe had done to Arya, she was finally going where she belonged, where she was fated to be.

"I love you, Arya Miller."

"I love you, too." She looked up at him for a few more seconds, soaking in all of his features one last time before turning to follow a complete stranger into the rich forests of Recensere.

Chapter 4

BEYOND THE VEIL

Arya tentatively stepped through the Veil and walked beside Finnigan, who had finally mastered walking like a Mortal, albeit a little wobbly. It took her a second or two to register the fact that it had *actually worked*, but when she finally looked up, her eyes were bombarded by a rush of color.

Everything there was colorful, every leaf and branch and flower painted with more hues than she had ever seen or known in her life in the Borderlands. Magyk filled the hole in her soul that she never knew was there, swirling around her heart like a warm summer breeze.

The trees towered high, their branches waving with life. Flowers glowed in the dark night, lighting the way through the inky black, and the sky erupted in a fit of foreign colors, dancing around like silk ribbons full of stars. Even the path seemed to have life in it. The stones shone with fresh moonlight and little fireflies flitted back and forth, their little bulbs strobing intermittently. Arya studied them, fascinated.

"Ye made it through the Veil after all." Finnigan stated after a few seconds, looking her over. "I wasn't sure for a second there, but here ye are. Welcome to Recensere. Me name's Finnigan, by the way."

"I'm Arya. Wow, is it always so beautiful here?"

"Well it—" Finnigan paused, chuckling softly at the awestruck look on Arya's face. "I guess I've always taken it for granted."

"There are so many colors..." Arya skimmed her fingers along a branch hanging in front of her. She'd never seen leaves look so alive before. "I," she giggled, trying in vain to count them all, "I don't even think I know all of their names."

"How could ye not—" Finnigan started a sentence, but quickly remembered what the world outside the Veil looked like. Aside from a few things, the Mortal village of River's End was filled only with brown. "Oh. Right." What a different life this girl had lived.

"What's this one called?" Arya pointed to one of the glowing Magykal flowers.

"Purple." Finnigan replied. "Some call it violet. Depends on who ye ask, I guess."

"And this one?" She cupped her hands around a firefly, peeking in at the colored light through the cracks in her fingers.

"Yellow. Like dandelions and daffodils." The Leprechaun grinned, watching her flit from thing to thing, taking in every detail she possibly could. Then, he sat down on a fallen log. "I'm sorry. Not used to these long Mortal legs. I'm feeling quite sore. Mind if we take a breather?"

"Fine by me." Arya sat down beside him and looked around at all of the moving things. Even the bugs here were beautiful. A butterfly with wings that looked like they had been crafted from stained glass fluttered by and landed on the end of the log beside her, pausing for a moment before flying off into the night, leaving a trail of glitter in its wake.

She had seen something similar in one of her mother's books, the books Katherine Miller wasn't supposed to have. When Arya was young, Katherine had taught her about all of the flowers that used to grow in the human village she grew up in inside the Veil before the Rebellion and everything else.

When Arya closed her eyes, she listened to the river babbling nearby, crickets chirping in the quiet night, the calls of all the wild things, the owls and the wolves and everything else. And when she opened her eyes, the world around her didn't disappear. This forest, living and breathing and filled with Magyk, was a real place, much too real to be a dream.

"So…ye didn't know ye were Magyk?" Finnigan asked tentatively. He wasn't sure if it was a sore subject or not. "I mean, from what I gathered…"

"No, I didn't. The blue eyes are new. All of this is so new. I'm guessing that for all of these years, the people in my village…my parents…they've been doing to me whatever they…did to you. I'm sorry."

"It's not your fault." He chuckled a little at the irony. "I guess we're both in new worlds."

"Yeah, I guess so." Arya nodded.

Finn looked her over and finally noticed the glowing thing around her neck. His eye for shiny things was not as good as it used to be.

"Where did ye get that?"

"Henry gave it to me. He found it. It's from somewhere in this place."

"I didn't think it looked Mortal." He stared for a while longer before tearing his eyes away from it. "I'd tuck it into yer dress when we get to my village. I may not have a Leprechaun's greed at the moment, but *they* sure as shamrocks do. For something that pretty, they might rip ye apart for it."

Arya's eyes widened as she slipped the necklace behind the fabric of her dress.

"Well, they might not tear ye apart, but they would come mighty close."

"Thanks for the warning."

Finnigan stretched his long legs, and after deciding that they were feeling less sore, he stood without too much trouble. "I think I'm okay now. Let's get to Clover Town before me mam loses her head."

Finn murmured mournfully after a long while. "It even affected me clothes…"

"What?"

33

"The stupid Mortal spell. Turned me favorite sweater brown."

"Sorry about that." Arya knew it wasn't her fault, but she felt the need to apologize for what the people of her village had caused. No, not just the people of the village; her *father* had been at the helm of this little project. If it wasn't for him, or Henry's father, for that matter, Finnigan wouldn't be in this mess.

She'd grown up surrounded by these people all her life. She had seen how kind and caring they could be, how connected her mother was to her, but now she wasn't even sure Katherine Miller was really her mother at all. Her eyes were wide open now, and she couldn't go back to being that blind, naïve girl, brainwashed into believing a life in the village was all she'd ever need.

Arya felt *dizzy* thinking about it. Or maybe she was dizzy for another reason. She stumbled off of the path and leaned against a tree, her palm pressed to the soft moss-covered bark. Sparkles filled her vision and her ears rang so loudly it drowned out the crickets' chirps.

Finnigan took a few more steps before he noticed she wasn't at his side anymore. "Woah there, love. Are ye alright?"

Arya shook her head and held a hand against her forehead, fist clenched so tight her knuckles protruded, white and strained. Her skull was pounding with pressure, sharp and twisting between her temples. She felt like everything was spinning, around and around like the children running around the maypole at the Festival, and it wouldn't stop. She leaned more on the tree, grabbing onto it for fear she would fly right off the surface of the planet.

"Arya, what's wrong with ye?" Finnigan put a hand on her shoulder, and she squeezed her eyes shut.

They widened a second later flashing a dozen different colors, red, orange, green, yellow, silver, violet, blue, and green again. A silver and gold substance began to leak from her right nostril and she shook violently, bleeding this unusual Magyk blood that even Finnigan didn't recognize.

And then, with a final jolt, Arya's eyes slid shut and she fell over, landing in the dirt with a soft thud. Finnigan looked her in a panic, brown eyes blown wide and his heart pounding in his chest. He took hold of her shoulders and gave her a good shake. "Arya? Arya!"

He didn't know anything about Mortal sicknesses, and he certainly didn't know anything about whatever was happening to her, but he knew who might. So, unsure of what else to do, Finnigan scooped her into his arms as best as he could and ran off in the direction of Clover Town.

Chapter 5
THE PROBLEM WITH ARYA

Finnigan wasn't quite sure what to do with the girl lying limp in his arms. The thick gold and silver mixture of what he assumed was whatever strange Magyk-tainted blood ran through her veins was still dripping from her nose and she was shaking in his arms, trembling fits overcoming her every few seconds. It was like the Magyk inside her had run up a fever to purge the filthy Mortal blood from her as soon as she had crossed over the border.

Perhaps she'd been too caught up looking around to notice it slowly progressing worse.

So he ran. He ran as fast as he could towards Clover Town, hoping beyond hope that the elders would know what to do with her. When he sprinted through Marshwood Grove and into Marshwood Clearing, all of the Magykfolk stopped to watch. Somehow, a Mortal had gotten through the Veil. Not one, but two of them. And one of them looked like she was dying.

"Mam! Mam!" he shouted as he reached the edge of the village, slowing down drastically once he was finally close enough to see it.

It was almost shocking to him, the sight of all of the little people no larger than his hand. They were so small. It had only been yesterday that he had walked down the little paths that would no longer support even half of one of his feet. The realization brought tears to his eyes, and he knelt on the ground at the edge of Clover Town so he wouldn't accidentally crush his friends and family underneath his giant Mortal toes.

"Mam, it's Finn." Tears streamed down his cheeks and his glossy eyes searched the village in desperation. There were a handful of confused Leprechauns assembling to look up at the two large strangers that had settled outside their village. "Mam, it's me, Finnigan. The Mortals...I was stupid and ventured outside the Veil and they caught me and...Mam..." Big wet tears dripped from his chin and onto Arya's still form.

"Finnigan?" A small curly-haired redhead wearing a long green dress walked out of a tiny house near the back of the village. The heels of her shoes clicked against the stone path and she looked up at the enlarged version of her little boy with tears in her eyes. "What did they do to ye?"

"I don't know." He shook his head. "They forced me tae drink this potion and the room shrank and...this is Arya. I think she's dying. I-I didn't know what tae do, Mam, I'm s-sorry."

There was a loud pair of clicks, and at the sound, the crowd of Leprechauns parted to make way for Elder Goldsmith. He was shorter than Finnigan's mother and leaned heavily on his cane, a finely-carved gold-engraved staff that had been a gift from the Fae of the Faerfolk Glade. He had a long red beard that was starting to gray at the ends, and he wore a green velvety top hat with a shiny gold buckle. His shoes, something he was the proudest of, had been made by the Elder himself, like all the rest of his shoes.

"Let me see the girl," he said, stepping closer to Finnigan.

Finn reached out and rested one of his large hands in the grass. Elder Goldsmith walked up onto his palm and let Finnigan lift him so he could see the sleeping girl with Magyk dripping from her nose. The flow had stopped, and her fits had calmed down, but she was still unconscious.

Bushy eyebrows furrowing, the elder asked, "Where did you find her?"

"In River's End. She saved me from the Mortals. I...thought she was one of them, but then she passed through the Veil."

"She crossed through the Veil...Mmm..." Elder Goldsmith scratched his chin and studied her for a few seconds longer. "And the Mortals did this to you, as well."

"Yes."

Then, without further explanation, the old man turned. "I'll be right back."

Finnigan gently lowered the old Leprechaun to the path once more and while his hand was on the ground, his mother stepped into it, motioning for Finnigan to bring her closer to his face.

Máire Ó Floinn looked up at her son with a weary smile. He was here. He was alive, which was more than she thought he would be after his little unauthorized trip to River's End. Many Leprechauns hadn't survived their journeys there recently, and now she knew why. The Mortals were playing a dangerous game, experimenting on Magykfolk like they were rats. If they weren't careful, someone much more powerful than her would have to teach them a lesson.

"Mam, I'm sorry..." He hung his head, great big tears falling like rain. She reached out to touch his freckled face and hushed her son. "I'm s-so s-sorry—"

"Finn, all I care is that ye got out of there alive. We'll fix this...Get ye back to normal. Whatever it takes." She rested her forehead against his for a moment, letting herself finally shed a few tears, and then she pressed the smallest kiss he had ever received above his brow. Finnigan smiled a weary smile and then set her back down on the path with the rest of the Leprechauns.

Elder Goldsmith emerged from his house just as Arya began to stir in Finnigan's lap. She didn't open her eyes, but she curled into Finnigan's chest. They had met a few hours ago and now, he decided as he looked down at her, he was stuck with her.

The elder had a scroll in his hands. It was very old, the paper yellowing and tattered, but Finnigan could feel its Magyk from where he was sitting. Goldsmith unrolled it and Finnigan caught a glimpse of the tiny words. He couldn't believe there was a time he had actually been able to read the lines of text that looked more like little dots. Being big made him feel so small.

Arya stirred again, this time opening her vibrantly green eyes and looking up at Finnigan, who studied her with a soft expression.

"Just listen," he whispered to her, tilting his head towards where Elder Goldsmith was standing.

Arya blinked a few times and nodded. Finn shifted her to a more upright position, and then Goldsmith began to read.

"There once was a girl from the Magyklands who fell in love with a Mortal." Goldsmith looked up, clarifying, "This was in a time before the Veil was cast, but tensions were rising." He adjusted his round glasses and continued reading. "The Mortal man belonged to a particularly mean-spirited village, so twisted by their jealousy of the beautiful Elf that they vowed to kill her should she ever step foot in their lands. The Elf wouldn't have that, however, and traveled far beyond the Borderlands south of the forests, all the way out to the Frynge to seek out the Magyk of a Wytch to make her Mortal."

Elder Goldsmith pushed his tiny little spectacles up his nose and cleared his throat. "The beautiful Elf, her hair and eyes darkened to a dull Mortal brown, traveled back to the village to seek out the Mortal man she loved. The two of them reunited, and she lived among the unsuspecting Mortals for the coming years. What the Wytch failed to tell her, however, was that the Magyk she'd been gifted was only temporary, and upon her fourth spring with the Mortals, its power had run dry. Because the Elf's own Magyk had been hidden away for so long, once it finally returned to her and fought off the power suppressing it, it also tore her apart, overwhelming her body until there was nothing left."

39

Finnigan and Arya sat in silence, watching as Goldsmith rolled up the scroll again.

"What do we do?"

"The Elf's fate could have been avoided had she found her way home, young one. Her Magykal bond with her own kind might have helped her repair what was broken by the Wytch's spell. She met her fate in a matter of days, but given that your Magyk was hidden from you for so long..." Elder Goldsmith stroked his chin, studying the very green eyes Arya was sporting. "I'd say you have about a Moons' Cycle to find your way. Any longer than that..."

"And what about me?" Finnigan asked, remembering that he, too, had recently had his Magyk suppressed.

"My guess is that it will wear off in time, Finnigan. Compared to Arya, the Magyk the Mortals forced on you...It's nowhere near as powerful. You should transition back to your true size soon enough, although nothing is certain; Magyk of this kind is rare and Wycked."

"Thank you." Arya exhaled a long breath. It was a lot to take in, but it was better to have answers than to go on unknowing. "I'll...I'll do my best to find my place, and if I do, I'll have you to thank."

The girl got to her feet slowly, wobbling in place. Finn watched her for a second, quietly thinking over his options. He looked at all of the little houses in his village, the little paths connecting them. He looked at his mother's tiny face, eyes glossy with tears, and then he looked at Arya, who was still finding her balance after her episode.

Finnigan Ó Floinn liked to think he was a nurturing person, a caring person. He wasn't as brave as some of the other Leprechauns, and he wasn't much of an adventurer unless there was some sort of treasure involved, but looking at Arya made him want to be. He knew that he'd regret it forever if he didn't at least try to help her.

"Where do ye think yer going?" The largest Leprechaun in the entire village, if not the whole kingdom, rose from his spot in the grass and stood beside her, immediately supporting her with a gentle arm around her shoulders. "Ye'd never make it out there without a guide."

Arya brushed a strand of hair out of her face and looked up at him, wide eyes changing from a bright Leprechaun green to a more subdued hazel-ish hue. "B-but you barely even know me."

"Ye saved me. I owe ye." He knew he was right. She had already helped him this far out of the goodness of her heart. He was going to get her home. After all, without her, he would have never made it back to his.

"Listen, lad." The elder tapped his cane against the path a few times. "Go to the Centaurs and ask them to search the kingdom for any families that lost a little girl around seventeen years ago. They can narrow down the search for you. Then head to Faerfolk Glade and ask them to look her over. They're healers, so they can at least give you something to stave off episodes like that one, maybe even stabilize you for a bit."

"Thank ye, Elder Goldsmith." Finnigan bowed his head. "Goodbye, Mam. Goodbye, everyone."

"I love ye, Finnie. I'll see ye soon." Máire wiped away a few stray tears from her cheeks as she looked up at the girl that had saved her little Finnie's life. "Thank ye for bringing my wee boy home…"

Arya smiled softly, nodding. "Of course. Let's hope he can help me find mine."

"Can ye walk, Arya?" Finnigan asked.

She nodded, but he still slung her arm around his shoulders as they left the little village behind them. When Finn looked back, standing between the trees at the edge of the Marshwood

Clearing, his town was no more than a cluster of twinkling lights.

Chapter 6

Arya and the Centaurs

Much of the walk to the Centaur camps within Marshwood Grove, Finnigan struggled as they traveled down the dirt paths. No longer was he springy and light, capable of skipping along on his toes. Now, he was forced to take Mortal steps. Heel-toe, heel-toe, as Arya had instructed him. It would be easier when they managed to find him some proper walking boots. His current foot situation, barefoot, was not doing him any favors. He yelled out every time he stepped on a sharp rock or a particularly stubborn stick.

The problem was that in the place they were going, none of the inhabitants had feet, and therefore, probably wouldn't have any spare shoes he could borrow.

Any of the onlookers watching them clumsily trek down the path would have sworn they were hiking home after a particularly smashing party at a Dwarven pub. After a while, though, the walking got easier. Finnigan fell into a rhythm of watching the path and avoiding the things that could hurt his vulnerable feet, all while supporting Arya's weight in addition to his own.

Finally, after the seemingly endless journey, they came across a large wooden sign written in the hoof-dug language of the Centaurs. Most Centaurs could read and write in the languages of many of the inhabitants of Recensere, given their job as the messengers and guardians of the land, but when given the choice, they preferred to use their own, even if it was difficult for their neighbors and guests to understand.

As the sun was beginning to rise and Recensere's moons started to blend into the rosy pinks and oranges of the sky, so rose the Centaurs, ready to assume their duties to the kingdom.

Andreíos, one of the King's appointed guardsmen and the General of the Centaur camp, stepped out of his cabin and hadn't even yawned or stretched when he noticed the Mortals standing at the edge of his territory. Immediately, he took hold of the horn hanging around his neck and blew into it. At the call, a small herd of Centaurs assembled and seized the intruders.

Arya didn't have the energy to fight back. Finnigan, on the other hand, was a fighter; he always had been. So, he writhed and kicked and squirmed in a failed attempt to break free from the Centaurs' hold, but the Centaurs were stronger than the Leprechaun-turned-Mortal and they outnumbered him heavily.

"Explain yourselves, Mortals." Andreíos crossed his human-like arms across his armored chest. A quiver hung from his hip and he had his prized bow slung over his shoulder. His helmet was still in his home, as he hadn't intended on having to defend anyone this early in the day, leaving his stern, strong face exposed. "How did you get through the Veil?"

"We aren't Mortals, ye arrogant beastie!" The Centaurs were taken aback at Finnigan's thick and distinct Leprechaun accent. "Let us explain before ye get yer saddles in a twist."

"Then explain." The Centaurs holding Arya and Finnigan slowly lowered them to the ground. Arya brushed the dirt off of her already grass-stained skirt and looked to Finnigan, but he motioned for her to tell the story of how they'd gotten there.

"My name is Arya. I grew up in a Mortal village called River's End. The people there...were experimenting with Magyk to try to keep me Mortal, but I'm not. They were suppressing whatever I really am."

"Elder Goldsmith sent us because if Arya doesn't find where she belongs before the end of the Moons Cycle, the Magyk that's built up will flood her system and kill her. We need yer messengers tae find out where she's from."

"Well, that explains your eyes…" Andreíos rubbed his stubble-covered chin as he looked down on the two teenagers, still sort of unsure of what to do with the situation. The Centaurs could look, yes, but if they were going to be of any help to this displaced Magykfolk, they needed to spread the word faster. A Moons Cycle was hardly enough time. "I'll send a messenger to the Square to dispatch the Ravens. They can spread the news faster than we can. And I'll make sure there's a decree issued in the Castle district."

"Thank you so much." Arya curtsied tentatively, unsure of how to interact with these magnificent creatures.

The world and social structure of the forests within the Veil were a mystery to her. Now she knew why the people of River's End shied away from the topic, all things considered. The less she knew about the world she was from, the less likely she was to want to visit it. That strategy hadn't worked on Henry, however, whose lack of knowledge about the rest of Recensere had only sparked further curiosity and wanderlust inside him.

"What colors have her eyes changed to?" The Centaur supposed it didn't matter all that much, given that they were in flux as she adjusted to the Magyk all around her, but it would be good to build a basis of the ground her Magyk had already covered. Perhaps some things could be ruled out.

"Blue, Green, and then just about all of 'em at once." Finnigan tried to remember if they had changed besides those, excluding her Magykal meltdown. "She's only been inside the Veil since a wee bit after dusk, sir."

"Okay. We can get you some supplies, but you should see the healers in the Glade soon." Andreíos reached down and pressed one of his large hands against the girl's forehead. She was indeed warm to the touch. "The sooner the better. I'll take you there myself after Kisa gets you settled. Come along." He motioned them onwards, further into the camp. The guards'

45

weapons were all lowered, but their expressions were still stoic and uncertain.

A few of the older parental Centaurs gently pulled children behind them as the strangers approached, their curious little faces peering out to see the strange Mortal-like creatures that had come to visit their camp. Arya studied the tall Centaurs around her. They had brown hair and blue eyes, not unlike herself at the moment, and the men sported thick facial and body hair, growing all over the Mortal halves of their bodies in dense patches. All of them wore their hair in long brown braids adorned with wooden beads and tied with red cords at the ends.

Andreíos seemed to be the most decorated, wearing shiny gold beads and golden cords at the ends of his braids. They stood out against his dark skin, almost glowing against the smooth surface. His bow was more ornate than the others' and his arrows had gold tips instead of red. It was evident immediately that he held rank there.

He trotted ahead of Arya and Finnigan, leading them to the largest dwelling in the camp. Inside the half-tent half-cabin structure, Arya noticed there wasn't very much furniture made for sitting. Instead, she spotted large piles of straw in the place where beds would be, which she guessed would be comfortable if she were half horse. In the kitchen area, just in front of the large space that made up the bedroom, there was a woman Centaur. Her braids were almost longer than Andreíos', and she, like him, wore gold cords at the ends of the elaborate twists.

"Kisa. We have visitors." Andreíos spoke softly, trotting forward to put a gentle hand on the woman's shoulder. Kisa, like the rest of the women Centaurs, was wearing a finely woven tunic on the top half of her body. It was light and wispy and moved with the breeze that drifted in through the sheets of fabric hanging in the doorway. Her face was warm and freckled and Arya found kindness in her eyes.

"Who have you brought along this time?" Kisa looked them over, and for the first time that day, Finnigan and Arya found someone who wasn't afraid of the two Mortal-looking people.

"Arya and Finnigan. It's a long story, but perhaps they can tell you after they get some proper rest." Andreíos walked further into the high-ceilinged dwelling and pulled out some feather-filled cushions and warm knitted blankets that he had picked up in his many years working at Castle Transverto. They were especially useful when he and his wife had guests.

"Thank ye greatly fer yer hospitality, and I mean no offence, but we don't have time tae…" Finnigan looked to Arya for support, but only found weary eyes with dark bags beneath them.

It had been a long day, and ever since Arya had crossed through the Veil, everything just felt…weird. It hadn't gotten any better after her episode outside of Clover Town. The aches swirling around in Arya's body were worse than any Mortal sickness she had ever caught combined. Maybe the Centaurs were right; some sleep might do both of them some good.

"You need rest, child." Kisa looked over the teenagers, her eyes full of maternal worry. "Don't concern yourself with the things to come, just take the journey as it happens and care for yourself along the way."

Andreíos and Kisa worked with Arya and Finnigan to set up a comfortable place to sleep. As soon as everything was settled, Arya and Finnigan climbed into the large mound of pillows and blankets and straw and found sleep in moments.

"I'll make them some soup and gather supplies." Kisa told her husband. She always seemed to be on the same wavelength as him, knowing just what to do or say to aid in the situation. She was a nurturer by nature, and having never had a child of her own, she cared for anything that would let her, Mortals and strangers included.

"I need to send a messenger to the Square to dispatch the Ravens. Urgent information. I'll explain when I return."

"I know you will." Kisa smiled softly as her husband pressed a kiss to her cheek and then trotted through the doorway and out into the camp.

Chapter 7

HIGH HEALERS AND SACRED SECRETS

When Arya awoke, she felt a bit better, but not tremendously. Her head still felt tight and there was a drop of silver liquid dripping out of her nostril. She wiped it away before the others noticed. It looked like Finnigan had awoken before she did, as he was sitting on a bale of hay at the dining table. She made her way over, yawning and stretching. He had woken up before she had, yes, but the dark bags beneath his eyes suggested he hadn't done much sleeping. She hoped he hadn't been up all that time worrying about her.

"Well, that's a new one." Finnigan tilted his head and looked from one of her eyes to the other, comparing the different hues each had taken on. "Ye've got one green eye and one blue."

"Huh." Arya nodded, sliding in beside Finn on the hay bale. Her leg brushed against his, and he scooted away the teeniest bit, giving her some room. "Odd."

"Your Leprechaun friend told me about what's happening to you." Kisa set a bowl of steaming stew in front of the girl and handed her a small wooden spoon. "No wonder you slept so long. Andreíos wanted to take you to Faerfolk Glade a few hours ago, but I told him to let you rest. You needed it."

"I did." Arya nodded gratefully. "Thank you."

"She's awake, I see." Andreíos parted the cloths hanging in the doorway and looked at the girl with the mismatched eyes. "Finish eating some stew and then I'll take you over to the Glade. The sooner, the better."

"Don't rush her, love." Kisa's voice was soft. She put a hand to Arya's forehead and hummed, frowning a bit before she said, "It does feel like you're running a bit of a fever, sweetheart. Are you feeling alright?"

"I have a bit of a headache, but I feel better than I did yesterday. Well, I guess technically, it would have been this morning."

"Good, good." Kisa smiled warmly. "Eat up, then. Wouldn't want your stew to get cold."

Arya melted under the show of affection. Kisa made her miss her mother. All things considered, Katherine had been hiding things from her, but whenever Arya had been sick growing up, Katherine was always the one who'd sat beside her bed, reading her stories and legends, singing her songs until she fell asleep. Her mother may not have told her the whole truth, but there had never been a time in her life that Katherine had ever mistreated her. All she'd ever received from the woman was kindness.

Now that she knew what she knew, really the only people in River's End she trusted anymore were Katherine and Henry.

Henry would have loved Recensere and all of the beautiful colorful things within it. Even though Arya was on a quest now, racing against the moons, she knew Henry would be better off beside her than he would be stuck in that village. With all of his knowledge about the kingdom and all of the creatures within it, he would have probably been a great help to her. Now, she wished she had listened to him more, tried to memorize all of the stories he told her, the maps he'd shown her.

Her fingers drifted over the spot where Henry's gift, the strange white stone, was hidden beneath the drab fabric of her dress. When he'd given it to her, she'd had everything she ever wanted: a life in the village with her best friend, and only seconds later, all of those plans shattered the moment her eyes turned blue. Part of her wanted to go back to that moment, to turn back time and go back to the way things were, live out the rest of her life in ignorant Mortal bliss, but part of her knew that this adventure was far from over. The fates wouldn't let her off easily.

Arya finished her stew and brought the bowl to Kisa, who was standing in the kitchen, chopping up vegetables. "It was really good. Thank you so much."

"Of course. You'd better get going. I'm sure Andreíos is waiting just outside. My husband isn't very patient, I'm afraid."

So, after saying one last goodbye, Arya and Finnigan walked through the doorway and back out into the Centaur camp to find the General.

In the time he had been waiting, Andreíos found a saddle lying around in one of the armories. He didn't use them very often. He used to, when the High Queen was pregnant and he had to take her somewhere outside Castle Transverto. That was back before the Rebellion, when tensions were still rising, but had not yet bubbled over and the royal family felt truly safe outside the Square.

Andreíos adjusted the saddle so it was sitting right on his hips and then motioned for Arya and Finnigan to come forward. Once more, the Centaurs of Hoof-Kick Camp all had their eyes glued on the two-legged strangers. Andreíos offered his large hand and helped Finnigan up onto his back and then Arya after. Arya sat sandwiched between the Centaur and the Leprechaun with the latter's hands tentatively holding her waist.

In all her years, Arya had never ridden a horse. She had ridden in the wagon of one once when her father had taken her out to the Frynge when she was small, which she was more or less sure had to do with one of the Wytches living in exile out there. Looking back on it, the fuzziness of those memories was answer enough.

But this was not like that at all. Andreíos raced through the forest, whizzing by like an arrow. He seemed to soar through the woods, trees blowing past like gusts of wind. When they finally arrived and he transitioned from a full run to a trot, Arya was in awe. Because she had slept the entire day, the sun was starting to set again and Recensere's moons were appearing in the evening sky.

Faerfolk Glade was nothing like she had imagined it to be. It was glittering, shining with so much light that even in the coming darkness, it didn't feel like night. It glowed like a rising dawn, full of warm Magyk and beautiful winged beings. Their power was like that of a million fireflies and just as yellow. The Fae flittered around the Glade, attending to their tasks and leaving trails of sparkling dust in their wake. Arya looked on with wide eyes. The creatures' wings looked like they had been woven from lace or silk, and they moved like they were underwater, weightless, graceful, like gravity didn't affect them at all. The sounds of twinkling bells and laughter and buzzing wings filled the quiet night as the sun sank lower and lower past the horizon, plunging the sky into an array of colors.

Finnigan watched Arya's reaction and laughed softly to himself, grinning. He didn't think he'd ever tire of how excited she got when there were new things. Of course, this would be her first experience with powerful, visible Magyk being performed.

"They're so beautiful..." Arya murmured, the ends of her hair lightening ever so slightly as she did.

"Aye, they are." Finn agreed.

Andreíos stopped at the foot of a huge tree. Its branches reached out every which way, long and strong and holding up what appeared to be a thousand little wooden birdhouses. As Arya dismounted from the Centaur, she noticed that they weren't birdhouses at all. They were little Faerie homes. Or rooms, at least. She doubted the small dwellings were big enough to hold an entire house.

Finnigan looked up, studying the Fae as they flitted from box to box, flying around glass jars that were suspended there too, refracting the light into dozens of rainbows.

In addition to healing and gardening, the Fae were also very good at adjusting their size. Some of them were smaller than Leprechauns and others were the size of Mortals, able to alter their height at will in order to interact with the rest of their Glade and the many guests that visited them.

"Faiya." Andreíos carefully studied the flitting creatures before spotting the one he was looking for. He waved her over.

She was blonde like the rest of them with clear blue eyes. Her features were sharp, her ears pointed, and her wings large and graceful, sparkling like a field covered in fresh morning dew. The Fae had rosy cheeks that sparkled under all of the lights, and when she smiled, a rainbow projected onto her skin from one of the jars hanging above her, casting her in an array of colors and making her look somehow even more Magykal.

"Is your mother here?" The Centaur asked.

More often than not, the High Healer was busy attending to patients or managing the Glade and could very rarely be caught flitting around like the rest of them. Her daughter, however, was always around, willing to lend anyone a helping hand.

"I can go get her." Faiya nodded and flitted off into the higher portion of the tree, changing her size as she ascended.

It seemed that when they were doing things on the ground, like tending to their expansive gardens, they grew to full size and when they had to retreat into their Tree of Life, they shrank in order to fit inside their miniature community. Arya found it fascinating.

Andreíos helped Finnigan and Arya down off of his back, and after a few moments, Faiya returned, another Fae beside her.

Faedella, Faiya's mother, was to the Faeries what Andreíos was to the Centaurs. Not quite their queen, but their leader, appointed by High Queen Allora however many years ago, the High Healer. Faedella was the most powerful Fae and was one of the elders that had woven layers of the Veil from Sun and Star

Magyk. She glowed more brightly than the rest of the Fae, and until she settled, Arya had to avert her gaze for fear of burning her retinas.

Faedella's wings were larger than every other Fae in the Glade, and they appeared to be crystalline, little patterns of what looked almost like ice covered her wings like patchwork. It reminded Arya of the thin laces Katherine used to hem all of her dresses with when she was a girl. They were intricate, but they were also powerful enough to carry the Fae's leader.

"Faedella, I have a favor to ask of you." Andreíos motioned for her to follow him further past the Tree of Life so they could speak privately.

Arya looked up at the giant glowing tree, trying to count all of the Fae. It was impossible, as every time she counted a handful of them, they would fly off and she would lose track, but she knew there must have been hundreds of them, buzzing around their home like a swarm of bees.

"Mortals?" Faiya stared at Finnigan, looking over his very brown hair and very brown clothes. "How did you get past the Veil?"

"We aren't Mortal, ye Fae."

"Is that a Leprechaun accent I hear?" Amusement lit up the girl's fair features, swirled with curiosity at the anomaly that was the mixture of something so familiar and something so foreign to her.

Finn answered her, "The Mortals beyond the Veil are dabbling with some transformation Magyk. Dangerous stuff. Arya here —"

Arya cut off the talkative Leprechaun with a sharp look. She didn't feel like talking about it.

"So, what *are* you?" The Fae floated half of a foot above the forest floor, her dainty feet covered in shoes that appeared to be made of leaves. Her dress was long and white, and looked like the fluff that flew from dandelions in the spring.

"If I knew that, I wouldn't have such a problem to solve." Arya's eyes, that had settled into a clear shade of blue, fixed themselves on the forest floor.

Andreíos and Faedella returned a few moments later, the Centaur trotting beside the floating Fae. Her clear blue eyes, framed by her thick eyelashes, looked over the not as Mortal-looking Mortal, taking notice that Arya's irises matched the shade of Faiya's and the tips of her long chestnut hair were beginning to turn a color that was honey golden. Almost the same color as the Fae. Almost.

Interesting.

"Arya, Finnigan, I'm going to come back tomorrow at dawn to give you the list my messengers are compiling of all of the places that are missing a child." Andreíos looked down on the teenagers, the *children* standing in front of him. As much as he wanted to accompany them further, he had a duty to his camp and the Castle. He couldn't just leave his post on such short notice. "The Fae are going to try to stabilize you and then you can get started in the morning."

"Thank you, for everything." Arya did a quick curtsy, the kind her mother had taught her to do in case she ever crossed paths with a prince.

The Centaur leaned forward and pressed his palm against Arya's forehead, a common way of saying goodbye in his camp and in the other Centaur settlements scattered throughout the kingdom.

"Until the dawn kisses your faces, two-leggeds." And with that, he was gone, galloping off through the woods at top speed.

Arya watched him run out into the twilight and felt a tug in her chest. Katherine, Henry, and now Andreíos and Kisa. It never occurred to her that the more places she visited, the more places she'd have to say goodbye to.

Once she was finished with her silent lament, Arya turned her attention back to the High Healer. Faedella floated closer to Arya and cupped the girl's face with both of her glowing hands.

Arya felt tingles run through her scalp and cheeks, down her abdomen and arms and off of the tips of her fingers. She raised her hand so she could see, and when she did, glittering light, not unlike the kind the Fae emitted, drifted from her fingertips.

"I don't believe you're one of us, child. If you were, we'd gladly welcome you home with open arms and open wings. I don't doubt you're from around these parts, though. The Magyk inside you blends with ours well, but not perfectly." Faedella spoke softly, maternally, as though Arya was another one of her daughters. It was the way she addressed all of the Fae in the Glade, with a level head and a warm heart. "But have no fear, we will find your home yet."

She released Arya's face and the new Magyk dwindled from a roar to a whisper. The girl still felt it there, drifting around her heart, but she couldn't summon it to her fingers again. So *that* was what Magyk felt like. Why, she wondered, did it feel so *right*?

Faedella looked to her daughter. "Faiya, take them to the in-firmary and then send the Circle to me so I can teach them the sealing spell."

"Yes, mother." She nodded and then flew off almost too fast for Finnigan and Arya to keep up. Luckily, it wasn't that far away, so they went their own pace and met her inside of it a few moments later.

"I'm sorry. I didn't realize how far you'd fallen behind until I turned around and you were gone. I suppose flying is a bit faster than travelling on foot." Faiya pulled apart some curtains, unveiling a pair of Mortal-sized cots that the Fae had built for the not-so-rare occasion that a larger creature from the other parts of Recensere might need a session with the kingdom's famed healers.

Arya sat on one of the beds, facing Finnigan as he sat on the other. Their legs dangled from them, Arya's feet kicking in a steady rhythm. Her eyes were focused intensely on a spot on the floor across the room and she chewed on her lip, a bad habit that often came to her in times when she was anxious.

"Nervous?" Finnigan softly inquired.

Arya nodded, exhaling a long breath. "Yeah. I don't know why. I shouldn't be. They know what they're doing, obviously, but—"

"But it's new. All of this is new. No one expects ye tae take tae it right away."

She smiled at that, nodding. "You're right."

Finnigan glanced out the door, watching, waiting, and then he looked back at Arya. The honey golden blonde had crept about halfway up the ends of her hair by this point, and maybe he was imagining it, but he swore her ears looked a bit pointed, too. "Well, do ye like it here?"

"I do. It's gorgeous, the people are so nice...everywhere, I mean. The Centaur camp, Clover Town, *here*...my father lied to me a lot, growing up. He told me the Magyklands were filled with—I don't know—monsters or something. He was so wrong. So, so wrong."

Finnigan smiled, and as he opened his mouth to say something in response, Faedella led the Circle into the infirmary.

The Circle of the Faerfolk Glade were the oldest Fae, the most experienced and therefore most powerful, under Faedella. There were six of them in total, and each of them wore a golden band around their right wrist. Setting Faedella apart from them was the golden tiara tucked into the braids on top of her head.

The Healers surrounded Arya, three standing on each side of her with Faedella at the end of the bed. They joined hands and the two closest to Arya took her rough Mortal hands in their own. It was quiet for a moment, the room dim. And then, very suddenly, there was an eruption of light Magyk. Cold seeped into the room, pricking up goosebumps on her arms, and a silhouette made of the glowing yellow Magyk of the Fae emerged from Arya's chest. It was a girl, running, her long hair flowing behind her as if blown by the wind. The Healers' eyes widened. In all their years combined, they had never seen anything like this before.

Arya's eyes glazed over with the rawest Magyk the elder healers had ever felt. It was powerful, and though they tried to break their grip and shatter the ring that bound them, they couldn't. They were forced to remain connected to the girl laying on the cot who seemed to be either completely oblivious to or taken over by this force.

Arya's lips moved but the voice that floated from her mouth was not her own. It was deeper. Still womanly, but deeper, more powerful.

"The Sacreds hold secrets untold, prophecies that were foretold."

Arya's body jolted and a drip of golden blood ran from her nose. Then, there was a burst of light and the ring was broken, the silhouette dissipating into a million little particles of Magyk before fading to nothing. Arya bolted upright and gasped, the blinding power rushing out of her eyes. Her breaths were ragged and desperate, as though she'd just been underwater for several minutes. She coughed a few times, hands clawing at her throat for a few moments until she finally looked around. Quiet, she took a few slow breaths, shaking.

Finnigan pushed through the line of Healers, careful to mind their wings, and took Arya's trembling hand.

"Breathe, Arya. Are ye alright? I'm right here."

58

Her hand clasped around his tightly, squeezing it a few times to ground herself in reality. For a second there, she felt like she was slipping off into space. "I-I'm sorry." Arya shook her head, centering herself. "I didn't mean to —"

"It wasn't anything you did, child. Fear not." Faedella walked around a few members of her Circle and pressed a hand against Arya's forehead, casting a weak sleeping spell on the troubled girl. "Sleep. I'll send someone to meet with the Sacreds and find out what it meant."

Arya nodded and leaned back against the pillows, her eyes shutting as soon as she touched the soft surface. Faedella took Finnigan by the arm and walked with him outside the infirmary into the brisk night air.

"I take it this isn't her first episode."

"She had one, a very different one, on the way to Clover Town. She started bleeding this shiny blood from her nose and her eyes flashed every color of the rainbow. Elder Goldsmith sent me with her to make sure...if something ever happened, I'd be there."

"Wise of him, as always." The magnificent Faerie rubbed her cheek thoughtfully. "We'll see what the Sacreds have to say, but... I've always been wary of them. They're much too Mortal to be Magykfolk, if you ask me. Do me a favor and keep an eye on her. When you leave tomorrow, if anything goes wrong...more people than her could come to harm. The Magyk in her is unlike any I've ever seen, no doubt scrambled by her time spent outside the Veil."

"Could be dangerous."

Faedella nodded.

Finnigan shrugged and grinned, and Faedella could have sworn she saw a brief flash of green in his brown eyes. "Well, I always wanted an adventure."

ENCHANTED INK

"So, they're, what, they're in the Fae camp?" Johnny looked to Selena. She was the only one that could read the book, and even though it hurt, she took it out and chipped away at the story within every day. So far, she had picked up on the fact that Arya's episodes were much like her own. The silvery blood, the flashing eyes, the twisting headaches.

"Well, they aren't *currently* there, Jonathan." Delphinus corrected from across the couch. "But they were, at one point, yes." He tried to seem casual, sitting there, but he wasn't quite adjusted to Johnny's living space yet. There were too many posters on the wall, the music from the speaker was too loud, and the light from the lamp in the corner of the room was far too bright. The entire space was a sensory overload to someone made of Starlight.

And though Johnny had turned off the music for the current gathering, the lamp and the posters weren't exactly something he could change at the drop of a hat. Not without his parents suspecting something, that was.

Johnny gripped a can of Pepsi in his large hand. He took a long sip from it before setting it back on the table, the metal clacking against the wood. His Letterman jacket and his faded black high-top Converse stirred Selena's memories, reminiscent of a time when they were just normal teenagers, back before her hair turned white and her eyes turned silver. Before episodes took over her every time something even *remotely* out of the ordinary happened in the odd, odd town they called home. Johnny could still be normal if it hadn't been for her. After all, she was the one who had Marked him.

"Don't think like that." Johnny said softly. He reached out and laid his hand on top of hers, intertwining their fingers. Their connection allowed him to peer into her thoughts every now and again. Not thoughts, exactly, no, her *emotions*. But after dating for a few years, he was usually able to tell what the cause of certain emotions were. "It's not your fault."

"It *is*, though. One or both of us are going to die because of my powers and the Prophecy and—" She sighed. "I'm not even halfway into this book and my brain hurts so bad from having to decode it. I just...I don't know how much longer I can do this..."

"Hey. We're gonna get through it together. Both of us. Alright?" Johnny's brown eyes locked with Selena's and he took her hands, raising both of them to his lips so he could press comforting kisses there. "The answers have gotta be in there somewhere. If I could help you, I would, but I can't read it. I'm here with you. Both of us are." He tilted his head towards Delphinus, who got off the couch opposite them and knelt down in front of Selena.

"I can try if you like," the white-haired boy offered softly.

Selena thought for a long moment before nodding and pushing the book closer to him. She held her head in her hands, the twisting, pinching pain finally flowing out of her temples. Johnny wrapped an arm around her and pulled her to his side. He pressed a kiss to her forehead and rubbed the tension out of her shoulders until he noticed that she was shivering. Then, he shed his blue Letterman jacket and wrapped it around her trembling frame.

His brown hair was a mess, yet even in the disarray, his mop still managed to look good on him. And his eyes were warm and kind, something that reminded Selena very much of Henry Miller. She had been reading the legends for about a week now and while she read the magic text, she could see everything as though it was happening in front of her, ancient history unfolding in her wake. Maybe that was why it hurt to read it so much. It felt like the book wasn't only a book, but a portal for her mind, transporting her to a place that had gone into Hybernation a long time ago.

Maybe there was a way to free the people there…

Maybe there was a way to break it…

Selena snapped out of it. This was what the book was trying to do, the reason it had been locked away to begin with. It was a powerful tool created by an even more powerful sorcerer. It was dangerous, and they had known that when they'd gone looking for it, but they'd exhausted every other option, so really, they didn't have a choice.

That was why she had taken her time, trying not to get too attached, but already, she felt its pull. And suddenly she didn't care about the pain anymore. She just wanted to be there again, to feel Recensere's warm embrace and powerful Magyk coursing through her.

"I'm okay now. Give it to me." Selena made grabby fingers and Delphinus obliged, his head spinning from trying to decode runes he couldn't understand.

"Just be careful, okay?" Johnny's voice was soft and full of concern. He knew his girlfriend was already so enthralled by the book that he feared when she finally finished it, she would vanish into its pages.

"I will." She pulled the book further across the coffee table and opened it again, its tattered pages flipping themselves until they landed on the spot she had left off. Selena felt the Magyk wash over her as soon as her fingertips made contact with the worn leather and then it was like she was gone, and Johnny and Delphinus were left to talk — or not talk — to one another until she resurfaced.

Chapter 8

A List of Lost Souls

At dawn the next morning, Finnigan waited impatiently for Arya to get up. Apparently, the sleeping spell Faedella had cast on her after her episode was stronger than he thought it'd be. So, to keep busy in the meantime, he organized their supplies, counting all of the food they had been given and making sure they got drinking water while they were still in Fae territory, where water was the cleanest. Next, he shined his new shoes and set aside the armor the Centaurs had left for Arya. It was much better than her grass-stained dress from the village, and it would hold up better in whatever conditions they were about to face.

During his visit earlier in the morning, Andreíos had brought some gold from Clover Town. The Leprechaun's whole home had come together and given as much as they could stand to lose, which was usually not much when it came to Leprechauns, but they knew their little Finn would need all of the help he could get to save the girl that had saved his life. As a Leprechaun himself, even in his Mortal form, he knew giving him this much...it couldn't have been easy for them to part with, which made him appreciate the gift all the more.

When Arya finally came around, Finnigan was on the ground under the Tree of Life packing everything they had into a few bundles of supplies that they could carry off to wherever the Centaurs' list told them they needed to go.

"Finn." The girl's voice was still thick with sleep. "Did the Centaurs come yet?"

"Andreíos brought some supplies earlier, but he hasn't brought the list yet, no." He shook his head and then stood up. It still made him uncomfortable that he was taller than her. Quite a bit taller than her, at that. Though now that he was thinking about it, he didn't feel as tall as he had been the day before. He wasn't sure. As much as he hoped this potion would wear off soon, he didn't want to be left defenseless if this little excursion lasted longer than he thought it would. "These are for you. Kisa found them in the armory while you were asleep. She thinks they'll fit."

"Thanks." Arya held up the leather garments, looking them over. The sturdy brown leather would protect her more than the thin cloth dress she was wearing. She went back into the infirmary to change. Just as she had gotten the trousers on and pulled the leather over her undergarments, she realized there were buckles and ties in the back that she couldn't reach on her own. It was then that Faiya floated into the room.

"I see you're finally awake. I'll inform my mother—"

"Could you—" Before Arya could even get the words out of her mouth, the Fae had flitted off to find Faedella.

Sighing, Arya reached around her back a few more times in a futile attempt to fasten the buckles and ties on her own. No such luck. How the Centaurs managed, she would never know. Perhaps they had longer arms than she did. She turned to the door and peeked outside, making eye contact with Finnigan, who immediately pretended he hadn't been staring at the door waiting for her to come back out.

"Finn, can you help me with the fastenings on the back? I can't reach them."

"Yeah, of course. Lift yer hair out of the way."

Arya turned around and pulled all of her long brown hair over her shoulder so it wasn't hanging in his way. He tightened all of the straps until they were comfortable, doing the best he could with his clumsy Mortal fingers.

"Does that feel good? Try stretching a bit." Finnigan instructed, letting go of the final buckle.

Arya crossed an arm across her chest, and then switched to the other one. She swiveled her torso both ways, adjusting to the feeling of wearing something so thick and form-fitting. "Feels good. Thank you."

Finnigan inspected her for a second, making sure none of her armor looked too tight or too loose. Arya looked up at the tall Leprechaun and reached to touch the tip of his ears, which were now coming to a bit of a point.

"Looks like it's starting to wear off," she told him, "a little bit, at least."

He nodded, chuckling before nudging her teasingly. "About time, really. I was afraid I'd be this big me whole life."

"Terrifying. Wow. I can't believe suffering a fate so horrible." She shook her head and rolled her eyes at him.

"Who'd want to be Mortal when there are much more interesting things to be?" He was mostly teasing her as he looked out at the horizon. The sunrise had filled the sky with a warm palette of oranges and pinks and yellows. It was a welcome sight for the beginning of a long journey, a good omen.

Finn wanted to say something more, but the thundering hooves of a small herd of Centaurs interrupted his thoughts. They were mesmerizing. Before his incident with the Mortals, he had avoided them for fear of being crushed beneath their powerful hooves, but now, he could appreciate them in all their majesty.

Andreíos led the group of three, the golden beads on the ends of his braids bouncing and catching the sunlight with every step. In his large hands, he held a scroll, the end of the rich cream-colored parchment secured in place by a metal bar with a pair of gilded handles. There was a braided leather string wrapped around its middle, tying it shut.

Arya was itching to look at the list of potential parents. One of those names held the answer to where she belonged, and then these episodes and all of the pain that came with them would be no more than a memory and she could finally adjust to her new life here inside the Veil.

Maybe she had siblings. Oh, her heart raced at the thought. She had always been an only child, but she had longed for siblings to play with. She dreamed of sisters to braid her hair, who she could teach to make wreaths of brown flowers, or brothers to catch fish in the river and to help her with the crops before the harvest. Older siblings to guide her and younger siblings to tell stories to.

"We searched far and wide, went to every province in Recensere to ask if there had been missing children in the last fifteen to twenty years. The Ravens brought some names, as did my messengers. This is everything we could find."

Andreíos handed the list to Arya, making sure she had a good hold on it before he let go. Kisa stood beside her husband, and on his other side was Andreíos' second in command, a younger Centaur named Agathon. He had shorter hair than the other Centaurs, and a thick layer of scruff lined his jaw. His muscled upper half was covered in the same sort of leather armor that Arya was now wearing, and a gold streak was painted across his cheek, distinguishing him from the other Centaurs that lived in their camp.

"This is Agathon, my second in command. He's agreed to meet the two of you at the Blackrock Inn, just outside the mines. Do you think you can make it until then on your own?"

"We should be fine." Finnigan nodded, skimming over the list of places the pair had yet to go. "Up until then, we won't have tae cover too much ground in between."

"The journey is long, but your hearts are strong. The rest is up to fate." Kisa spoke, and the Centaurs' leader look at his wife in adoration. This wasn't the first time the two of them had guided adventurers and they were sure it wouldn't be the last, but she was still finding it hard to say goodbye. She always did. There was maternal pain hidden behind her wise words.

"Thank you, for everything." Arya rolled the scroll back up and loaded it into her pack with shaking fingers. She knew it was a mistake to look into Kisa's warm gaze before they left. Arya's eyes fogged with tears in response. How could she possibly thank people who had given her so much? "I don't know how I could ever repay you for all you've done for me."

"There's no need for that, child." Kisa hushed her, brushing the brown hairs out of the front of Arya's face with a gentle hand. "We serve the Kingdom of Recensere and all of its creatures. No matter where you belong, you are one of our own, and we would have it no other way."

Each of the Centaurs gave Arya and Finnigan one last goodbye, pressing their palms to the young two-leggeds' heads. Then, Faedella wished them luck and waved her hand over them in a blessing. The assembly watched with weary eyes as the two walked down the path and off to their next adventure, hoping beyond hope that they weren't already too late.

Chapter 9

TROUBLE IN THE STILLGREEN FORESTS

According to the list the Centaurs had given Finnigan and Arya, the nearest place they were set to visit was a patch of thick woodlands called the Stillgreen Forests. There was said to be a family of Satyrs tucked into Faun's Knoll there that had lost a daughter around eighteen years before. It wasn't too far away.

Finnigan, who knew the forests much better than Arya did, insisted that this leg of the journey would be over by the time the sun was beginning to set. Maybe even shorter, as his calculations were based on a time when he was a bit smaller in stature.

Arya tried not to, but she was beginning to ration her days. She didn't want to spend too much time in one place or traveling from one dot on their map to another. The more ground they were able to cover, the more they would be able to rule out. It was a process of elimination, after all, and if they failed to travel fast enough, it would prove to be deadly.

Finnigan explained that the province they were in, the western portion of Recensere, was mostly forests and woodlands. Out further east was where you ran into the deserts and places like Coppertown, where the Tynkers lived. The Leprechaun told her that they had once lived in a town called Kettylvale, but it had been drowned out by the floods that turned Ravenglow Forest into Ravenglow Swamp, now a common place for the Ogres and Trolls to gather. After the destruction occurred, Spyrits had taken to the Ruins of Kettylvale and refused to leave, so no one really went there anymore, and the Tynkers moved somewhere warmer, where floods were less likely to occur and rust their appendages.

Up in the north stood the Northern Mountain, the December Woodlands unfolding at its feet. It was the home of the Wynterborn and some of their chilly companions that could stand the cold. To the south of Recensere lied the Borderlands, where Arya was from, and beyond that, the desolate Frynge.

So, with a rough schedule sketched out, the two ventured down the path until they came upon a sign. It was lying on the ground, obviously knocked down by something. Finnigan picked it up out of the bramble and tried to read the letters, but it was obscured by a sticky, slimy green substance. Grimacing, he wiped his hands on his pants.

"That's disgusting."

"Yeah," Arya agreed, "What *is* it?"

"I'm not sure. I don't remember hearing about any giant snails in these parts, but ye never know." Finnigan shrugged. "I've learned new things every day since I met ye." Finnigan squinted straining his eyes to make out the letters under the thick layer of grime. He could just barely tell that the sign said the Stillgreen Forests were further down the path they were on. "This way, I think."

So, they continued on their way, not taking notice of the occasional rustle in the bushes or the way their boots slightly stuck to the stone. Nor did they notice how dark it was getting because of the thick patches of trees until Arya found herself wishing they had a lantern.

Arya moved to lift her foot, but it was stuck to the path. As was her other one when she tried to pick that one up instead.

"Finnigan—"

"I know, mine too." He tugged at his leg and lost his balance as he got his foot free from his boot. Yes, his foot was free, but the force of doing that task toppled him over onto the path, thick with what he now realized were webs.

This was not good.

"Finnigan!" Arya shouted as she watched the Leprechaun struggle to free his entire body from the sticky trap that held him there. His cheek was stuck against the cobblestones, fingers spread wide, splayed against the road. His right leg, the one that still had a boot on its foot, was pinned beneath his left leg.

"I'm alright," he lied, voice muffled from his awkward position on the ground.

"Can you try to get free?"

"I don't know if ye can tell from there, but it seems I'm stuck." Finnigan tried to turn his head so he could see Arya standing behind him, but immediately regretted it when he felt it still stuck to his cheek, pulling at his skin. "Ow, ow, ow, not working." He wiggled his fingers, currently the only part of him aside from the top half of his face that he could move. "Can ye come over here and help me up?"

"My boots are stuck, Finn. If I try to go over there, I'll get stuck, too." Arya looked around for someone, anyone to help, but they were in the middle of the dark forest alone. To make matters worse, she spotted a pair of glowing red eyes out in the distance. "Uh…"

"What's wrong *now*?"

"There's…" she lowered her voice, "*something out there.*"

Arya took in a deep breath to shout for help, but before she could, she felt a sharp pain in her neck. She reached up to slap the spot, but as she raised her hand, a tingling numbness spread through her arm, and then through the rest of her body until finally, she collapsed onto the path, her head landing on Finnigan's thigh and her eyes slowly closing.

"Arya!" he cried, but a few moments later, he felt the sting pierce the middle of his back. Though he tried to stay awake, he couldn't. He couldn't fight the poison coursing through his blood. It forced his eyelids shut, and his body fell into a deep and heavy sleep…

Arya came awake first, her head hurting something fierce. She tried to move, but her arms and legs had been bound together with the sticky stuff. The *webs*, she realized.

A chill ran up her spine.

These must be the terrifying Spyders her father had told her about, the ones that feasted on unsuspecting creatures who couldn't defend themselves. She felt something squirm against her and looked over to the source of the motion. Finnigan was bound beside her, the side of his body pressed against hers. She exhaled a breath of relief. For starters, he was alive, which was good.

Finnigan let out a groan, stretching as best as he could, given their predicament, and then opened his eyes to see exactly what mess they'd landed in.

"Spyders," he deduced. "The spinners capture anything they can get their hands on. We had a good run, Arya, but we're done for. They'd eat a Leprechaun like me as an afternoon snack. You might get lucky and make it to dessert."

"Maybe not." Her eyes spotted something shiny glint near her foot. Their bags were shoved up against another tree, but it appeared that her knife had fallen out in the Spyders' rush. Now, if only she could reach it.

Against another tree, there was a Faun, no, a Satyr, bound by webs like they were. He was just beginning to come around, his eyes blinking a few times as he tested his binds. He wasn't so much scared as he was frustrated. Arya guessed that maybe this wasn't his first encounter of this kind.

"You're alive over there?" the Satyr asked.

Arya nodded. "At the moment, yeah."

"Well, let's try to keep it that way, eh?" The Satyr nodded to a third tree, where there was an unmoving bundle of whatever the Spyders had previously killed. Their face was covered in webs, obscuring their identity. "I've been here before. If we're too loud, they'll hear us. The only reason we're still alive is because they're probably still out hunting. We have a chance."

"They're not too far." Arya looked for a moment like she was somewhere else. Her eyes flashed red and then faded to a solid black. She didn't seem to have pupils or irises. Just inky black coating her eyeballs, the exact opposite of what had happened in the Faerfolk Glade.

Finnigan looked at her and immediately regretted it, shuddering when he saw her eyes take on a new, terrifying form derived straight from his nightmares. Well, he wouldn't get *that* image out of his head any time soon. If, for some cruel reason, Arya belonged here of all places, he'd have to break off their friendship.

"What?" she asked. "Are you okay?"

"I'll tell ye later." He shivered. There hadn't been Spyders on the list. But then again...who in their right mind would have wanted to ask them anyway? And additionally, what Mortal was crazy enough to kidnap a Spyder's child?

"I have a knife on me," the Satyr told them, eyeing Arya nervously, a bit startled by the sudden Spydery flash in her eyes, too. She didn't seem like one of them. She *couldn't* be one of them. But if her friend had jumped... "I'm going to cut myself free and then come over there, alright?"

"Just hurry up, would ye? We're already on borrowed time," the Leprechaun snapped.

The Satyr struggled against the bonds for a few seconds, and then Arya watched as the glint of the knife emerged from his webbed bundle, slicing the sticky strings. He stood on his hooves, pushing through the cocoon of death and emerging.

His top half was human, covered in a cozy-looking red sweater, and his bottom half was that of a goat. The fur covering his legs matched the rusty copper-colored patch of wild curls sprouting from his head. Deer-like ears stuck out from the auburn curls, and a pair of short horns barely poked out from above his forehead.

He trotted over to the wads of web Finn and Arya were trapped inside and worked quickly to cut Finnigan free from the binds that held him before turning his attention to Arya. Finn helped the girl to her feet. Her eyes were still shadowed in black, but she seemed to be unaffected otherwise, just a little stirred.

Then, without warning, her previously nonexistent irises flashed red and she stood in a protective stance in front of the other two.

"What's wrong with her?" the Satyr asked the Leprechaun.

"It's a phase." He shrugged. "She has them sometimes. It'll wear off when we get out of here."

"We have to get out of here *now*." She looked up at Finnigan and grabbed their stuff. Arya shoved Finnigan's pack into his arms and plucked her dagger out of the webbing on the ground.

The Satyr motioned the other two on, but failed to look in front of him. There was a Spyder there, its spindly limbs poised and ready to strike. Arya, whose instincts seemed to be a lot quicker now than they had been in the past few days, pushed him out of the way into Finnigan's arms, and raised her dagger, eyes glowing red. The Spyder's eyes flashed an identical shade and then it shrank away, not in any rush to anger the girl with a knife aimed at its neck.

"*Leave, girl. And take your friends. We'll eat yet.*" The Spyder glared at her, hissing, but didn't attack further.

The boys looked to Arya for an explanation.

"Didn't you hear her?"

Finnigan shook his head, eyes wide and limbs trembling.

"...She said we can leave." A chill ran up her spine at the thought that she had understood this creature and the other two hadn't. She had to get out of there, and fast.

Luckily for the trio, the settlement of Satyrs they were looking for wasn't far from there. The Satyr that had saved them, whose name they learned was Pollux, lived in the very village they were trying to get to.

"So why exactly are you travelling through Faun's Knoll? We don't get very many visitors, these days."

"We're actually looking for a family of Satyrs." Arya pulled the list out of her pack of things and read off the name. "The Castorians."

"Well in that case, Pollux Castorian at your service." He gave a little bow and tipped his imaginary hat. "Might I ask why?"

"I'd rather not talk about it until we're inside."

Pollux watched in awe as Arya's eyes changed from solid inky black to a vivid green color. There was Magyk in her, he could tell, something powerful. He'd heard of Magyk like that when he was no more than a little Satyr, before his horns had even grown in, but he'd never expected to see any with his own two eyes.

Pollux led Arya and Finnigan further out of the darkened woods to where the sun shone through the trees. It felt good to have the warm light on her skin again. She wanted to soak it up like a sponge after being trapped in a place that was so dark and cold and hopeless.

Finnigan was still brushing off little strings of webbing that he had missed. Though he tried not to think about it, every time he closed his eyes, he saw Arya looking at him through a Spyder's eyes. Her slight changes in eye color had been subtle until this point, not really something you would notice unless you knew what was going on inside her, but seeing what had

74

unfolded in those woods was something his little Leprechaun heart could barely handle.

He shook his head, pushing the spine-chilling thoughts out of his head. After all, there was nothing worse she could be than a Spyder. Any other creature was an improvement.

The trio crunched through the bramble and fallen leaves for what seemed like ages until they came upon the twinkling lights of Faun's Knoll. It was a little bit darker outside than when Arya and Finnigan had departed from the Faerfolk Glade. The sun was due to set soon, and Arya's heart sank as she realized that another day of the Moons Cycle had passed and she still wasn't any closer to finding her home. The clock was ticking. She didn't have forever.

Pollux raced up the path to open the door of his cottage, welcoming Finnigan and Arya inside with a warm smile and a slight bow. They walked inside, leaving their sticky muddy boots in the doorway as to not track filth all over the vibrant rugs covering up the cobblestone floor like patchwork. It was a nice house, warm. The inside was colorful and quaint. One of the walls was filled with books and the carpeting was soft under Arya's stockings. Pollux rapidly stomped his hooves on the welcome mat, generating little thumps like that of a dog's leg hitting the ground while itching its ear.

"This is my house. My parents used to live here, but they moved to the Square a few years back..." Pollux sat on a chair by the fireplace and motioned for the other two to sit. "Now, what business do you have here? Does this have to do with the Centaur that came by yesterday?"

"My...name is Arya. I'm from River's End. It's a village just outside the Veil. My...parents, as it turns out, are not actually my parents. I was taken from somewhere in the Magyklands when I was a baby, but we don't know where from. I was given a list of all of the families they could find that had lost little girls in the past eighteen or so years. We came here to find out if this was the place I once called home."

As she spoke, Pollux watched her chestnut brown locks become more of a copper color at the tips, curling slightly. Her eyes changed from green to blue, like his own, but he didn't notice any other changes. Just subtle things that made her a little more like him, but without the hooves or doe-like ears.

"My sister...was lost when I was just a wee faun, maybe six years old. She was just a youngling then, barely able to tottle along, and she was taken. Her name was Asteria, after the goddess of the stars. We think the Spyders made off with her, but we were never really sure. One moment she was playing in the meadow, a few feet from me and my mother, and the next she was gone. My parents left for the Square because they just couldn't face the memories and guilt of losing her anymore." He studied Arya, tears threatening to spill from the glistening cerulean of his eyes. He smiled softly, shaking his head and chuckling as he wiped away the tear rolling down his cheek. "But if you *were* Asteria, we'd welcome you back with open arms."

Pollux reached out and rested a hand over Arya's. She felt tingles run up through her arm and down her spine, but nothing as potent as she had felt before. She felt connected to him, yes, but probably not in the way they both hoped. Pollux was the first potential brother of hers, possibly the first of many potential siblings out there waiting for her to come home. This was the kind of thing she had always wanted, a sibling, a friend, a real family that loved her for her.

Arya's heart sank a little as it settled in that this was not her place; this Magyk was not the kind that was tearing her apart from the inside.

"Who else is on your list?" he asked, taking his eyes off of the girl.

Finnigan moved to get the scroll out of Arya's bag. It was larger than he remembered. Shaking his head, he handed it to the Satyr so he could look it over.

"Quite a few names, eh? How do you plan to narrow it down?"

"Well, when I find my place, I'm supposed to revert back to normal, whatever normal happens to be for me. But if I don't find home by the time the Moons Cycle ends, the Magyk inside me will kill me."

"Can't you make the Mortals tell you where they took you from?"

"If ye had seen what they did to me, that wouldn't even be a question." Finnigan shuddered at the thought. "I'm a Leprechaun. Or I'm supposed to be."

"I could tell from the accent. They made you Mortal? I didn't think they were capable of that sort of thing. Not without some powerful Magyk, at least."

"I didn't think so either..." Arya sighed, looking out the window of the cottage. Dusk was falling on their first day and she had barely made any progress. Just another dead end and a close encounter with some wicked weavers that would have gladly made her into a meal if her Magyk hadn't dabbled in theirs.

"You're welcome to spend the night here." Pollux spoke softly. "And I wish you luck on your journey. Hopefully, it won't take you too long to find where you belong." There was sadness in his eyes.

Arya felt bad for raising his hopes only to let him down when he realized his sister hadn't come home after all, that she was just a stranger accompanied by the unluckiest Leprechaun in the kingdom.

"Thank you." Finnigan nodded. "You look tired, Arya. Why don't we get some—"

Arya's eyes went wide. Finnigan reached out to touch her and a flash of pain tore down his arm. He ripped his hand away and watched as a drop of silver dripped from her nose. Her eyes flashed brown and then blue and then silver.

"H-Henry..." she murmured, her voice swallowed up by the chirps of the crickets outside the window.

In her mind, there was a flash. She *saw* him. She didn't know why or how, but she saw him and she knew deep in her soul that he was going to do something unbelievably stupid. She knew his schemes, the way his plans worked, and if there was any reason he thought Arya was in danger, he would find a way inside the Veil so fast...

But how would he manage something like that?

"He's going to do something stupid. I can feel it." Arya snapped out of whatever vision she was caught up in and looked at Finnigan with worry in her eyes, as though he could make it better.

"It's nothing, Arya. It's just the Magyk playing tricks on ye. Get some rest." Finnigan pressed his hand to her forehead. It felt warm.

Pollux looked at the girl, concerned, eyebrows wrinkled in confusion. "Does this happen...often?" he asked. In all his years living in the Magykal woods of Faun's Knoll, he'd never seen an episode quite like that one.

"Often enough," Finnigan replied. He got Arya to lie down on the couch and draped a blanket from one of their supply packs over her. She closed her eyes and was out instantly, exhausted from the white-hot flash of power she'd just endured.

"Is she okay?" the Satyr asked, his voice so quiet the Leprechaun could barely hear him over the crackling fireplace.

"I don't know." Finn tried to ignore the hitch in his voice, the way his eyes felt like they might fog up with tears at any second.

A piece of her Magyk had woven itself into his heart and now that she was struggling, it hurt him too.

So, he busied himself and studied the map, plotting out where they had to go next. The nearest place to where they were was the Isle of Highland, where the High Elves lived. Oh great. Well, that would be an adventure for the next day.

Pollux helped Finnigan set up a cot in the corner of the room, where he could watch Arya, should anything go wrong in the middle of the night. Once he took off his armor and pulled one of the Satyr's knitted blankets up to his shoulders, he stared at Arya for a few quiet moments. Her eyebrows were knit together in her sleep, but she seemed alright otherwise.

On his way out of the living room, Pollux blew out the lantern on the wall, the fireplace down to gentle flickers of flame, and in the dark room, Finnigan finally surrendered to sleep, dreaming dreams of the many things to come.

Chapter 10

The Isle of Highland

The next morning, Arya awoke to the smell of fruits and veggies sizzling on the Satyr's stove. She'd had quite a bizarre dream about Henry, something about winter, or maybe a snowman. She couldn't remember it now, though. With her eyes open, her dream was long-forgotten.

Pollux was standing over the stove, stirring the food with a wooden spatula as it cooked. An apron was tied around the Satyr's waist, and she noticed a blue woolen scarf hanging around his neck.

"Good morning, Arya." Finnigan got up from the table and helped Arya take a seat beside him. "How are ye feeling?"

"I'm okay, Finnigan. I'm not made of glass, you know." If he was already acting like this after only a few days, what would he be like when it got closer to the end of the Moons' Cycle? Arya knew she shouldn't think like that, that if all went well, she'd find her family long before her hourglass emptied, but even now, her hope was beginning to dwindle.

"I know that." He nodded. Finnigan rested a hand over hers. "I know. I'm sorry. I'm just...worried, is all."

Finn looked different this morning, Arya decided. He had some more of that Leprechaun skip in his step. The ends of his brown hair, very slightly, had the faintest hint of red in them, and his eyes were starting to look more hazel than they were brown, closer to his natural green. His ears were even more pointed now than they had been the previous morning and he seemed to be a smidge shorter too.

Finnigan had noticed it before she did, taking stock of himself in the mirror hanging on the wall before she'd woken up. And while he liked that he was starting to feel more like himself again, he realized that this inverted transformation would only hurt them in the end. As he became less Mortal, Arya would start to descend into a state of flux that would eventually kill her if they didn't find her home in time. As they'd seen the day before, there were dangerous things hidden in the beautiful forests, but how would he be able to fight them when he was half a foot tall?

He remembered, though, that Agathon would meet up with them eventually, and then he didn't feel so panicked about it. They were lucky to have help from the Centaurs. At this point, they needed as much of it as they could get.

Pollux turned his head to glance at Arya over his shoulder. "Your Leprechaun friend told me you're headed to Highland today. Good luck with those High Elves. Tricky, those ones. Elitists. They don't really like anyone that isn't an Elf. Rumor has it they almost left the kingdom a few years back when their High Lady tried to challenge the King. It didn't go so well, so she tried to bury the incident altogether." Pollux shook his head, plating up the caramelized fruits and vegetables before setting a serving in front of Arya and Finnigan and then in front of himself.

On the table, there were little bread rolls and a jar of red jam, which reminded Arya of Henry. Though, when she tried it, she found that this was even sweeter than the jam in the village of River's End. Henry would love it. She made a note to herself to bring some back to him whenever she finally saw him again.

Once breakfast was over, Finnigan and Arya packed away all of their things, and Pollux walked with them outside his cottage.

"Are you sure you two will be alright?" He asked, his kind blue eyes glimmering in the light of the rising sun. "I wouldn't be able to stay with you for very long, but—"

"We'll be alright, Pollux. Thank you for everything."

"No, thank *you*." Pollux took one of Arya's hands in both of his and looked down at this girl who was, he was sure, very close to the girl his little sister could have grown up to be. It was bittersweet, sure, but he wasn't sure he wanted her to leave his life just so soon. He glanced over at Finnigan. "If it wasn't for the two of you, I'm not so sure I would have escaped the Spyders' webs in one piece."

"Glad we could be of service." Finnigan chuckled. "Take care."

"You, too." Pollux looked out at the horizon, his copper curls waving slightly in the breeze. "If you leave now, you should be able to make good time." He studied Arya one last time. "Stay safe, young one. I hope you find where you belong."

Arya nodded, tears fogging her vision the tiniest bit. "I hope so too."

So Arya and Finnigan set out on their way. It was a long journey, one that would took them concerningly close to the Crypt of Hallows. Finnigan set Arya at ease by telling her that the Necromancers tended to keep to themselves, but she was still wary; they were shunned by the rest of the kingdom, sure, but had not yet been banished to the Frynge. It was bound to happen sooner than later, really inevitable at this point, and yet, they were still around, raising skeletons to dance through the woods whenever they pleased.

The Leprechaun changed the subject, not wanting to scare the girl more than he already had. Instead, he told her he figured they could hire a ferry to take them to the Isle once they got to the Elven Lands. It wouldn't be too hard to convince someone to take them, hopefully. He was just hoping Arya could keep her episodes under control until then. No one would want to take her out onto the water if they knew how unstable she was.

So, they kept walking, boots crunching through the fallen leaves until the dirt path changed to stone. Finnigan told her a few tales from his childhood, reminiscing about when he was just a wee little Leprechaun, a mere babe in a village of people who were five inches tall.

"I was around seven when I saw me first squirrel. I was terrified of them, their beady eyes, their squirmy tails. Still am, a wee bit."

"Squirrels?" Arya giggled. "But they're so cute! They only eat nuts, I think. And they're friendly, if you don't get too close."

"Yeah, right, try telling that to a Leprechaun, Arya." Finnigan shook his head, chuckling.

"I guess that would be different when you're five inches tall…"

"Six inches, thank ye very much! Tallest in me entire village, I'll have ye know."

"Well yeah, of course you're the tallest in your village *now*."

"Oh, hush, you." Finn laughed and elbowed her, sending Arya into another fit of giggles. It made him happy to see her happy, even with everything that was going on inside her.

But the talks of height did bring back memories. When Finn was little, Máire had tracked his growth on a door frame with a little piece of coal. He remembered how eager he had been to mark his new height every time he sprouted up a few millimeters. It felt like a lot to him back then, but being up here made him realize just how small he really was, just how little each of his inches mattered in a world of thousands of miles.

He didn't say these things to her, though. Finn just continued to walk beside her, smiling softly.

The closer they got to their destination, the more Arya's thoughts began to wander to the possibility of her family, what they looked like, where they were. She must have gotten her nose from *someone*. Back in River's End, aside from her hair and eyes, she never really resembled either Katherine or John, and now she knew why. Instead, someone else was responsible for her dimples and her freckles and her smile.

Arya didn't know what she would have done if she was in her family's shoes, if a Mortal had taken her child without her ever knowing why or when or how. It was a scary thought. How does a parent stand losing a child? How do they go on in a house with an empty room, an empty bed, an empty chair at the table?

It must tear them apart.

The Mortals may have taken her to love or raise or whatever they had convinced themselves they were doing to her, but they had stolen something from her that they couldn't replace, that *she* couldn't replace, and she didn't know if she could forgive them for it.

Finnigan and Arya came upon the border to the Elven Lands by midday. The division was marked by an arch made from stones and a great wall of thorns dividing these fresher, greener woods from the woods outside of it.

Fortunately for them, the Elves inside these gates were much nicer than the ones residing on the Isle of Highland. You see, the Elves that inhabited the majority of the Elven Lands, the Wood Elves, were considerably more welcoming than their Elitist cousins, the High Elves. Many citizens of Recensere saw no real division between the two, which continued to be a source of frustration for the Wood Elves, who wanted no more than to tend to their lands, trade with their neighbors, and benefit the kingdom as best as they could.

Arya looked to the Leprechaun for guidance. All that was standing between them and the Elves within was a gate, manned by a dark-haired Wood Elf in a green hood. Taking the cue to lead the way, Finnigan took a few steps forward and cleared his throat, pulling the attention of the gatekeeper from the scroll sitting in his lap.

"What brings you to the Elven Lands today, travelers?" The Wood Elf looked over the visitors warily. They were filthy, boots caked in mud and dirt, leaves caught in the girl's hair, webs clinging to their clothes. Wherever they'd come from, it didn't look like their journey had been pleasant.

"We're here by order of the Centaurs, sir," Finnigan explained. "It's a wee bit urgent."

"I can see that," the gatekeeper stated, looking them over once more. The Elf motioned to someone they couldn't see behind the wall of thorns, who pulled a lever. Wood clacked together along the fence as a contraption whirred to life and the doors of the gate opened, allowing Finnigan and Arya to step inside.

The Elven Lands were nowhere near as intimidating as Arya expected them to be. The dark-haired Wood Elves walked along the wooden paths and small bridges that arched over shallow streams. Towering trees watchtowers, inside which there were Elves with binoculars, carefully monitoring not only the woods beyond their border, but also the sea on the other side.

Dozens of people roamed around the settlement, hauling nets full of fish up from the beach, chopping wood for their fires, tending to their gardens full of vegetables and herbs. Fruit-bearing trees grew beside the wooden dwellings the Elves lived in, and there was a woman picking lemons from a tree in the house nearest to the gate, a few small children playing in the grass at her feet.

Finally, in the center of the Elven quarter of the forests, there stood a large fortress made from stone, smoke billowing upwards from within its walls. Tips of branches peeked out from over the top, their emerald leaves shimmering in the wind. This was where the gatekeeper led Finnigan and Arya. He signaled one of the guards standing on either side of the entrance of the fortress and they lowered their weapons.

Inside it, there stood a large throne made from branches, planted at the foot of a magnificent tree that reminded Arya of the one standing in the Faerfolk Glade. In the center of the fortress was a large bonfire, glowing ashes floating up to the heavens. A few elves tended to the fire, adding dead leaves and bits of waste. Inside the shelter of the vast branches was the man Arya could only assume was the leader of the Wood Elves. His long black hair was arranged into several intricate braids, a crown of leaves settled into the thick tresses. The edges of each leaf were tipped in gold, the telltale sign thus far that he belonged to the higher end of the Elven hierarchy.

Once he noticed that someone had entered, the leader sat at attention, studying the foreigners that had walked through the gates. They did indeed fit the description he was given.

"And you must be who the Centaurs sent. I am Elion, General of the Wood Elves. Welcome to the Elven Lands." Elion rose from his throne, adjusting the long green cape that was draped over his shoulders. "I trust you got here safely."

"For the most part." Finnigan looked to Arya, who shrugged.

"We made it in one piece."

Elion nodded and took a few steps closer, his bare feet peeking out from under the length of his tunic. "I'm glad." Once he was standing in front of them, Elion asked, "Finnigan, you're from the southern woodland district, yes?"

"Aye, sir." Finnigan nodded proudly. "Clover Town in the Marshwood Clearing."

"Right, then, do you happen to be familiar with the Recenserean laws pertaining to Halflings?"

"Of course, sir." The laws had been written shortly after the Leprechaun was born, due to the Mortal Rebellion, as many

Mortals had fallen in love with Magykfolk over the years, result-ing in the creation of Halflings, a species that was not quite Mor-tal and not quite whatever Magykfolk they were mixed with. Halflings were allowed to live within the Veil, of course, as they had Magyk in their blood, but they were not always treated kindly due to their Mortal heritage.

"And you're aware that they're legal, yes."

"...yes, sir. If I may ask, why wouldn't they be?"

Arya watched as frustration worked its way across the Elven General's features. His irritation didn't seem to be pointed to-wards her Leprechaun friend, though, instead focused on an-other force the girl was sure he would explain.

"I'm glad you asked. You see, our cousins across the pond over there went about spreading a rumor a few years ago that Halflings were illegal while their staff was getting low. These days, their beautiful castle is filled with Halfling servants who work for them in return for the High Elves' supposed 'protec-tion.'"

"That's not right." Finnigan's features twisted, eyebrows furrowing as he mulled over the new bit of information. "Can't the King and Queen intervene?"

"The King and Queen don't know. The kingdom is under enough stress as is, what with murmurs of a second Rebellion afoot. This would only make matters worse, I'm afraid." Elion shook his head. "And we have no physical proof of the matter aside from a few stray murmurs that have slipped from their compound. They've closed their doors to us, but by order of the Centaurs, they have to let you inside."

"I think I see where this is going..." Arya nodded. Unfamil-iar with the politics of this world, all she could do was absorb the information being presented to her. She trusted the Wood Elves because *Finnigan* trusted the Wood Elves, but she was sure the High Elves had another side of the story.

"I won't send the two of you alone, of course. My son, Daenys, will accompany you. It's Lorelei's weekend with him anyway." Elion motioned another Elf to come forward. Previously, he had been tucked away under the great tree, hidden beneath its vast shadows.

The son of the Elven General was unlike the other Elves wandering about the Elven Lands. Rather than a head of thick black hair like his father, or the fair platinum blond of the High Elves, Daenys sported a mix of both, dark streaks scattered among his sun-bleached golden ones, making him look like salt and pepper. The varied locks were cut a lot shorter than the rest of the Wood Elves' long braids, and they hung in the boy's eyes, almost long enough to keep Arya from seeing that even his irises were split, one of them a brilliant turquoise the color of the Recenserean seas and the other as green as the foliage that surrounded them.

"I suppose I'm taking you to meet my mother, then." Daenys shot a tired look towards his father before turning his attention to the foreigners in front of him. "This way."

The son of the Elven General led the two out of the stone fortress and into another structure in the camp. This building was smaller and had several racks of cloaks and tunics, not unlike those the other Elves around the camp were wearing. Daenys took two cloaks and two tunics out of the large supply and handed one to each of them.

"I know my mother. She'll probably have you change out of these anyway, but she'd much prefer Wood Elf tunics to the muddy armor you're wearing."

"Thank you." Arya nodded and looked over the shimmering tunic and the long green cape.

Daenys left the two of them in the little hut and they hastily changed into the new outfits, each of them hiding their exposed forms behind rows of hanging capes. When Arya emerged, Finnigan watched as the length of her hair darkened to match Elion and the rest of the Wood Elves. Her brown eyes had taken on a green hue as well, and when she tucked a lock of inky strands behind her ear, he found they'd come to a subtle point.

"Oh, Lorelei is going to *hate* you." Finnigan smirked, and Arya looked at him in panic.

"Why? Did I do something—?"

"No, but you look like a Wood Elf and she hates Wood Elves."

"All set?" Daenys poked his salt and pepper head into the hut, doing a double-take at the sight of Arya's altered features, and then shrugging. It wasn't really his business.

"Ready." Arya told him, and Finnigan nodded in agreement, taking a step closer to her.

Daenys motioned them forward and they left the hut, setting out down the wooden paths through the village. Arya mulled over Finnigan's words while they walked. If Lorelei did *indeed* hate Wood Elves, what did that mean when it came to her son?

There was a thick line of evergreen trees dividing the Wood Elves' camp from the coast of the Iridescent Sea. Not a single cloud blotted the clear sky, and from the beach, Arya could make out the Isle of Highland, the towers of its golden castle gleaming in the sunlight. She was taken aback for a second at the sight of it; she'd heard tales of great glittering palaces as a child, but until now, they had been little more than stories to her. She never thought in all of her days that she would ever see one with her own eyes.

Looking up at the large castle, she wondered how someone had even managed to steal someone from this fortress of an island. It was extremely guarded. But maybe the increased security had been a result of whatever had happened before, the reason the High Elves had lost a daughter.

Finnigan spotted something standing on the docks that was a long way from home: a Troll. So the Elves were hiring Trolls to do their dirty work now. Bouncers, of a sort, meant to keep anyone who didn't belong on the island out. Daenys didn't look fazed, however, as he brushed past Arya and Finn and walked right up to the Troll.

"I SMELL MORTALS! ON MY BRIDGE – ER, DOCK!" The large creature roared. There had been a long rainbow bridge there before, Finnigan remembered. And oh, how Trolls *loved* to guard bridges. But, they would settle for a dock if need be. "LEAVE!"

"I'm as much High Elf as they are Mortals. Let them pass." Daenys rolled his eyes, unamused by his least favorite of his mother's toys.

"I DIDN'T HEAR ABOUT NEW HALFLINGS COMING TO THE ISLE!" The loud Troll informed them.

Finnigan grimaced and wiped a few stray splatters of *he didn't even want to know what* off of his face.

"Well too bad, Grogg. Our new friends here are crossing by order of the Centaurs. It's out of our hands."

The Troll's face contorted in confusion as he thought about it. He huffed a couple of times and then grunted, frustrated. "YOU CAN'T TELL ME WHAT TO DO!"

"Of course I can't," Daenys shook his head, smirking the slightest bit as he threatened, "but do you remember what happened the last time I told my mother you wouldn't let me cross to see her."

Surprisingly, at the mere mention of the High Elves' leader, the Troll paled and stepped aside, allowing Finnigan, Arya, and their Elven hero to walk further down the lengthy dock. It seemed Lorelei was the one person that could instill fear in even the biggest and toughest creatures. That wasn't reassuring in the slightest.

"YOU CAN PASS. THIS TIME. BUT DON'T THINK I'LL LET YOU BY THE NEXT TIME WITHOUT A GOOD REASON!" He rumbled at the three.

Finnigan gripped Arya's hand, intertwining his fingers with her own and then pulling her towards the ship that was waiting at the end of the dock. Another Elf, this one a High Elf about Daenys' age, sat inside it, waiting.

"Daenys." The High Elf noted with disdain, his nose wrinkling at the sight of the Elven Halfling.

"Orris." Daenys replied with equal contempt. "I see mother has you rowing boats now. An improvement from sitting on your throne all day."

"An assignment that will end as soon as I escort the three of you across the waters." Orris motioned them inside the boat. Daenys stepped inside first, offering a hand to Arya to help her aboard, and then Finnigan.

Before the Leprechaun had even settled in all the way, Orris snapped his fingers and a current picked up, carrying the fine golden ship across the waters and causing Finnigan to just about topple over into the water.

Orris guided the boat to the front of the castle, where there was an elegant gold-encrusted entrance with a grand staircase, statues of Hallowyngs and Elves scattered around a large fountain that spewed misty water. Sunlight caught in the little droplets, casting rainbows on all of the shiny surfaces. Arya, a girl who grew up surrounded by brown, had never seen so many colors in one place before. Studying them, she doubted she even knew all of their names.

Once the boat had glided up to the center of the landing where the staircase stood, Orris stopped the boat with a flick of his wrist, some secret Magyk Finnigan didn't know the High Elves had.

Daenys was the first to step onto the sandstone, helping Arya up after him. Something had changed about her, even since they'd gotten into the boat. Her hair was still darkened like a Wood Elf, yes, but now her irises were such a clear turquoise that the color rivaled the hue of even his mother's eyes. When she tucked her inky locks behind her ear, he noticed the tips of them had come to a point as well, the Magyk inside her molding her to fit the shape of the people around her.

And yet, when she looked up at him, nodding gratefully, it didn't seem like she'd noticed the changes at all, let alone caused them. Her state of flux was something subconscious, innate. Daenys found it fascinating.

"I've never seen this much gold anywhere in me life..." Finnigan mumbled, getting up out of the boat next to Arya. His knees had turned to jelly, his eyes to saucers as he took in the sight of the largest collection of shiny things his little Leprechaun heart had ever laid eyes on.

Arya looked up at him and waved a hand in front of his dilated pupils. He blinked a few times, snapping out of the trance. "You can look, but we shouldn't touch," she warned.

"Right. You're right." Finnigan nodded and took a breath in a feeble attempt to ground himself. This castle was indeed shiny and big and beautiful, but it also belonged to the High Elves, who were sure to have his head if he took so much as a pebble.

Another High Elf, this one a woman dressed in a silver tunic with her platinum hair braided back away from her face, bowed to Daenys and then to Orris, addressing them before the visitors standing in front of her.

"Prince Daenys, Prince Orris, your mother would like to speak with you while I see to our...guests."

Prince? Arya looked to Daenys for an answer, but he only rolled his eyes.

"Of course she does." He exhaled and shook the hair from in front of his eyes and turned to Arya. "Don't worry too much; they mean well. I'm sure I'll see you soon."

And then he was gone, he and Orris walking through the gilded front gates and leaving Arya and Finnigan with the other Elf.

"I am Haela, the Queen's advisor. I'm to make sure you're dressed..." she looked over their Wood Elven garments with a scowl, "*properly* to meet with her."

There it was again; Haela was using royal honorifics with people Arya was fairly certain were not the rulers of Recensere. If Arya knew anything more about the politics of the kingdom, she might have spoken up, but instead, she elected to stay silent. The last thing she wanted to do was start a war.

Haela escorted the pair through the glimmering halls. The floors were shiny, made from a sort of rainbow-colored marble that Arya doubted had been easy to come by, even in a place as colorful and Magyk-filled as Recensere. She was fascinated by the way the light and colors reflected off of the golden walls. A few High Elves walked here and there, casting judgmental looks on Arya and Finnigan as they passed.

Further down the hall, the "Queen's" advisor opened the door to a large bedroom.

"Put your belongings in here. We'll get you properly washed and dressed for the Queen," she told them. Arya and Finnigan set their belongings on the edge of one of the beds and then followed her back into the hallway. She motioned Arya into one room and Finnigan into another.

Waiting in the room, there were several kinds of Recenserean creatures Arya didn't recognize immediately. Some had features that were sort of similar things Arya had heard of, but they didn't quite fit the descriptions Henry had given her.

Halflings, Arya realized, these were the Halflings Elion had told them about. They weren't dressed in silver like the other High Elves in the castle or in golden tunics like the one Orris was sporting. Instead, these Halflings were dressed in drab brown rags, not unlike the kind Arya had stumbled through the Veil wearing.

"You're the stranger, aren't you?" asked the first Halfling quietly. She was Mortal aside from her Faun-like ears and her deer-like nose and the slightest tint of copper in her hair. "The one here to see the Queen about the lost child?"

"I am." Arya nodded.

"Where did you find her, the lost child?" asked another Halfling, walking to Arya and helping her take off her cloak. She realized that these Halflings, the handful of them that were here, would have to see her undressed. It made her nervous to think about; no one had seen her completely undressed aside from her mother in River's End. Her face flushed red at the thought.

"I *am* her. Or, I might be. I came here to find out."

"I've heard of the people like you." The third Halfling had the ears, eyes, and glittering skin of a Fae, but the brown hair of a Mortal. "The people who change."

"What do you mean, 'the people who change?'" she asked, and as she did, her eyes settled from their turquoise blue to a forest green instead.

"Your hair was almost black when you came in. It's a lot lighter, now," the Faun chimed. She took Arya's very muddy boots and pinched them between her index finger and thumb in an attempt not to get her hands dirty. The Halfling couldn't imagine what the girl in front of them had been through until this point, but she had bits of web in her hair that might be a struggle to get out until they got her into the water.

The Halflings helped remove the rest of Arya's Elven garments and got her into the warm waters of a golden bathtub. It

94

was bolted down to the floor, resting against the wall behind a privacy divider. There was enough room in the little space for the three Halflings to surround Arya. The process involved a lot of scrubbing. Arya's hair was lathered, rinsed, and then lathered again at least three times. One of the Halflings was busy rubbing the dirt from the bottoms of her feet and cleaning underneath her fingernails while another was still teasing stubborn bits of web out of her hair.

After what seemed like hours, which was probably true of the whole process since orange rays of sunset were shining through the windows of the room, Arya was finally out of the tub and dressed in a silken robe. Her feet were bare, and for the first time in a long time, Arya felt genuinely clean.

One of the Halflings left and returned not too long after with a golden evening gown, the end of which flowed against the marble floors. The Halflings helped Arya into it, tying the corset tight around her waist. She found it hard to take in an entire breath, but the Halflings assured her it was supposed to feel this way.

They put her rapidly lightening hair up into an elaborate series of braids and finished the look with some mysterious sprays and a tiara encrusted with gemstones the Halflings told her came from the Blackrock Mines, where the Glowyr, known to some as the Dwarves, and the Goblins lived. They put her feet in sparkling slippers and patted her features with sparkling dust that made her glitter like a Fae.

And then another High Elf dressed in silver came to get her.

Arya followed her down the halls of the castle and into a grand dining hall. An Elf she could only assume was the aforementioned "Queen" sat at the end of the table. Her chair was the largest and her features were the fairest. Around her head was a glittering crown, similar to, but much larger than, the one the Halflings had put in Arya's hair.

"Ah, here she is at last." The Queen held out a hand and motioned Arya over to where she was sitting. There was an empty spot beside her. The rest of the long, long table was occupied by other High Elves, Daenys, Orris, and Finnigan, who was also dressed in golden garments. His hair had obviously been dyed red, as there was still the tiniest bit of evidence hiding in his hairline, and he wore a nervous expression on his face.

The Queen took Arya's hand and studied her intently, memorizing each little detail.

"Calloused hands," she noted. "They worked you in that village, didn't they? No amount of pampering could get rid of this piece of your past, I'm afraid."

"Right." Arya almost felt ashamed at this stubborn piece of herself that wouldn't go away. Everything else was changing, and yet this hadn't.

"Stand for me, darling. Let me see you."

Arya stood up, as did the Queen. She spun Arya around, smiling brightly as her turquoise eyes looked over the girl. Yes. She was exactly as she thought she would be.

The Queen smiled confidently and looked down the length of the table. "Attention, Elves. Let it be known to all that at long, long last, our princess has finally come home."

"P-princess?" Arya stuttered.

Finnigan's eyes were as large as hers were. The Leprechaun watched as even more blonde streaked through Arya's hair, still pulled back into an updo.

"Mother, that's absurd —" Daenys attempted to interject, Orris' face also contorting in confusion.

"Princess Fraeya, I am your mother, Lorelei."

"M-mother…" Arya stammered, dumbfounded. She looked at the beautiful woman in awe.

This Elven "Queen" acted so certain that Arya was the one she lost, so positive that this was their princess returned to them.

Arya smiled, but it didn't feel right. A piece inside her still doubted that the journey was this easy, that the road ended here.

"Mother, this couldn't *possibly* be…" Orris trailed off, looking at the girl who was very much *not* his twin sister.

Lorelei ignored the concerns of her sons and instead turned to Arya. "My child, sit, enjoy the feast and then get some sleep. Tomorrow evening, we'll celebrate your return with a grand ball." The Queen sat back down in her seat, and with a little hesitation, so did Arya.

Finnigan nudged her foot under the table and gave her a look, asking wordlessly if she was alright. She nodded, silently promising herself she would visit his chambers during the night to talk to him about her doubts.

The meal was incredible, consisting of mostly grilled fish and herbs and other vegetables that they had grown on the isle. There was a creamy clam soup loaded with potatoes and sparkling drinks that fizzled, sharp on Arya's tongue. Dessert was a frozen cream decorated with sweet berries and rich, colorful sauce.

After dinner, Lorelei spent a few hours introducing Arya to the other Elves. Finnigan retired to his room early, figuring he'd take advantage of the fluffy bed and blankets for as long as it took these high and mighty Elves to kick him out of this castle that he very obviously did not belong in. He figured that if this was *indeed* the place his friend belonged and he had gotten Arya home after all, he had done his job. Now, all he had to do was wait out the Magyk that was keeping him Mortal and return to Clover Town. Easy-peasy. And then, his life could finally go back to normal. He drifted off dreaming of rainbows and fields full of gold.

As soon as the excitement was over, the Halflings helped Arya change into a soft nightgown and took her light blonde locks out of the tight braids holding them back, leaving them in loose waves that cascaded down her shoulders. She sat on the bed for a few moments, listening while the Halflings' footsteps retreated down the hall. Once she believed the coast to be clear, she plucked the golden lantern hanging by the bedroom door off of the wall and crept the opposite way of the footsteps, following her memory to the room she and Finnigan had taken their stuff to earlier.

She knocked on the door a few times and waited. There were faint footsteps on the other side, a sleepy groan, and then—

"Who do ye think ye are, knocking on—Oh, Arya. I mean, *Fraeya*. Princess." The Leprechaun did a sleepy bow, his newly red hair strewn every which way. His accent was even thicker when he was half asleep.

"'Arya' is fine." She sighed, walking into the bedroom.

He closed the door behind her. "Ye alright, princess?" Finnigan managed a sleepy lopsided grin. "What're ye doing out of yer chambers at such a late hour?"

"Do you really think this is it?" Arya asked. She busied herself with studying the carvings on the headboard of Finnigan's bed. It was ginormous and softer than a Hevynrealm cloud.

"I don't know. Lorelei certainly seems to think so."

"Yeah, but Daenys doesn't. Neither does Orris." Arya fiddled with her fingers, pointed ears burning red as she waded deeper into her thoughts. "How angry do you think she'll be if I don't really belong here?"

"Probably angry enough to run us from the island." Finnigan shrugged. He took a seat on the vast mattress and patted it, inviting the troubled girl to join him. "You feel it, don't you?"

"I know I belong somewhere, but it's not here." Arya admitted it to herself, too. She didn't know how belonging somewhere would feel, but she knew it wouldn't feel like this.

"We'll stay for the ball and then we'll steal a boat and row back to the Elven Lands." Finnigan took her hand gently, looking over at the would-be princess with a mischievous grin on his face. "Don't ye worry one second. We Leprechauns *always* have an escape plan."

Chapter 11

ESCAPE FROM THE ISLE OF HIGHLAND

By the time the sun came back up, Arya and Finnigan had everything arranged for their escape. They had gotten their belongings down to the servant entrance, where the Elves kept some extra boats. They weren't as gilded or grand as the boat that had brought them to the island, but they were buoyant, and that was really all that mattered.

Once she went back to sleep, the false princess awoke to a breakfast of grilled salmon garnished with lemon juice. On the side, there was a little cup of raspberries and a note from Lorelei.

"Glad to have you home, Fraeya. I'll be showing you around, today. I hope you enjoy your breakfast!

-Mother"

Arya sighed, taking a moment to look at her reflection. Even after a whole night on the isle, the roots of her blonde hair were still brown. One little piece inside her was resisting the change, and that meant she didn't belong there, no matter how desperately Lorelei wanted her to.

It wasn't Arya's fault Lorelei had sprung the whole princess thing on her without waiting to see if she was the real heir to the Elven throne. Although, that didn't stop Arya from feeling guilty about it.

The Halflings arrived to dress Arya in another golden gown later that morning. This one had a golden corset and the skirt was flowy and white and iridescent like rainbows in the sunlight. She was going to miss this, especially when she was back out in the Recensere woodlands trekking through dirt and mud and whatever other dirty, dirty things the journey introduced her to.

She'd only been there for a day and she was already thinking like a High Elf. Since when had dirt and grime ever vexed her? Never. Not after the upbringing she had in River's End. A little bit of dirt makes the flowers bloom, even if the flowers are brown.

Arya needed to leave this place and fast.

Finnigan came to her room while she was waiting for an escort to take her to see Lorelei. He was dressed in another golden suit, tailored to match the dress she was wearing, and he had a cape of glimmering rainbows trailing down his back.

"Good morning, princess." A lopsided grin tugged at his lips as he approached her, brushing a strand of blonde Elven hair out of her face. "Looking less like yerself these days."

"Believe me, I know." Arya sighed. "The girls put my hair in braids so tight I'm afraid they'll pull my brains out of my forehead."

"Probably want them to last all day. They'll be looser by tonight." Finnigan adjusted her tiara and she chuckled as she realized that the boy standing in front of her had more braiding knowledge than she did. An image popped into her head of Finnigan, sitting in his little meadow surrounded by all of the younger Leprechauns in their little green dresses waiting for him to braid their vibrant red hair. "That's a good color on ye."

"What, gold?" she asked.

As soon as the words came out of her mouth, she remembered that despite his height and his High Elven clothes, he was still a Leprechaun. He was naturally attracted to gold. Very much so. In fact, it was the reason he had found her village in the first place. So, being there, in a castle made of it, couldn't be easy for him. She had noticed more than a few times now that his eyes tended to wander to the shiny crown sitting in her hair. There was no way they were taking it with them. She had already let this little charade go on long enough.

"Compliments yer features."

Arya smiled softly under Finnigan's warm gaze. His eyes seemed to be slightly greener than they were brown now. She still had to look up at the Leprechaun, but now it was only by a few inches instead of almost an entire foot. In a few days' time, she had a feeling he'd be at her eye level. It was kind of odd, how fast he was shrinking.

A knock on the door pulled Arya from her thoughts.

"Come in." Arya called confidently. She had this fake princess thing down.

"So that didn't exactly unfold as planned..." Daenys walked in the room, finally free of his mother and able to meet with Finn and Arya in private.

"You're telling me." Arya huffed in relief, her shoulders going slack when she realized it was Daenys coming into the room, and not one of the High Elves she had to convince of her "royalty" for one more day.

"About that, '*yer highness*' can ye explain what's goin' on here?" Finnigan crossed his arms and took a step closer to Arya. "Why are the Elves usin' the titles reserved for the High King and Queen?"

Daenys thought for a second before replying with a shrug, "To put it simply, my mother is insane and my father doesn't know how to deal with her without involving the *actual* King and Queen."

Arya nodded, processing for a moment before asking, "And what exactly does that mean for me?"

"She's trying to pass you off as my half-sister. It's not true. Fraeya died when we were only children, some sickness she caught. She'd just rather believe her fully High Elven daughter is alive than relinquish control of all Elves to me when I come of age."

"Ye'd do better than both of yer parents combined."

"Wait, why—" Arya began, but Daenys was quick to cut her off, realizing that since she had grown up in the Borderlands, of course she wouldn't have any idea of Recenserean politics, certainly not the drama surrounding the Elven corner of the kingdom.

"In High Elven society, leadership always falls to the firstborn daughter. And then, if there isn't one, it falls to the eldest son. It's not like that with the Wood Elves, but she'd rather not have me rule over both halves of this sector if she can help it. Reuniting the two halves of my family is the last thing she'd want."

"So I'm a pawn, then."

Daenys gave Arya an apologetic nod. "When it comes to my mother, a lot of people find themselves in that position, I'm afraid." The son of the Elven "Queen" turned back to the door, cracked it open, and then his expression changed from suspicious to annoyed. He reached outside the door and pulled his eavesdropping half-brother into the room by a pointed ear. "I knew it."

"Ow! How do you always do that?"

"There are perks to my condition, Orris." Daenys shook the black and white bangs out of his mismatched eyes. "What do you want? What did you hear?"

"Enough to know I'm not the only one who believes our mother has finally lost her mind."

Daenys' expression went flat. "Her mind is something she lost a *long* time ago, brother."

Finn crossed his arms and looked at Daenys. "Well, do ye have a plan or not? We don't have a lot of time on our hands to get Arya to our next stop."

"Oh, I have a plan. The two of you need to get out of here and fast."

"That, we can agree upon." Arya nodded.

"Tonight. After the ball. Any sooner and mother will go insane." Orris reasoned.

"That was our plan, too."

"Great. It's settled, then. I'll arrange for some of the Halflings to accompany us. They're all the proof we need." Daenys focused his mismatched eyes on the corner of the bed as he thought over what this meant for his day's schedule.

Obviously, he didn't want to ruin the strange relationship he shared with his mother, and if he brought any other incriminating evidence back to his father, she would surely never forgive him for it. But smuggling out a few of her illegal servants couldn't be too hard. They could testify against her in the King's court back in the Square and he would never have to get involved. Yes. This was a good plan.

"Proof?" Orris' eyes narrowed. "Proof of *what*, exactly?"

Ah yes, Daenys realized, a hitch in the plan. "Don't be dense, brother. You know as well as I do that mother twisted the truth about the Halflings."

Daenys' younger brother stared at him for a long time, silent before nodding in acceptance. It seemed he was learning all sorts of new things about his mother today. "I know we don't often see eye to eye," Orris started, meeting his brother's gaze, "but I trust you to do what needs to be done." Once Daenys nodded, Orris turned his attention to Arya. "Well, *Fraeya*, for the next several hours, it appears you're my twin."

"Wonderful."

"We should leave you. One of mother's advisors will be here any second to fetch you, I'm sure." Daenys looked to Orris, and then to Arya and Finnigan before leaving the princess' chambers.

"Well that was…" Finnigan exhaled a long breath, his freckled cheeks puffing out.

"Yeah." Arya let herself slump onto the bed, running her fingers along the intricate patterns of the soft comforter she was sure she'd miss while she and Finnigan were camping wherever they wound up next.

The mattress sank under Finnigan's weight and warmth enveloped Arya's hand as he took it in his own. She wasn't quite sure how she had ended up waist-deep in Elven politics, but if she had to get involved, she was glad she had Finnigan by her side.

There was a knock on the door. "Your highness, the queen requests your presence in the throne room." An Elf dressed in silver opened the door and looked in on the princess and her visitor. "I suggest you lovebirds not try anything until *after* the ball. Castle is on high alert at the moment."

"We're not—" Arya abruptly let go of Finnigan's hand, motioned between herself and the Leprechaun, and shook her head. "Finnigan is a friend. Nothing more."

"Of course." The Elf grinned a sly but unconvinced smile. "She said your...*friend* could accompany if he wishes. If not, there's plenty to be done in preparation."

"I'd like tae stay with the princess, if that's fine with ye."

Arya and Finnigan followed the Elf down the halls and into the throne room. Every person they passed on the way there turned to look at Arya and her companion fondly. It wouldn't last for long, though; they would find out sooner or later that she didn't belong with them.

The throne room was much larger than the dining hall that dinner had been held in the night before, and as Arya had been told, this was the space the ball was to be held in. Lorelei was seated on the largest throne, her back straight as a board and a professional smile on her face. Yes, "professional" was a good word for it, Arya decided. Not warm or kind; it didn't reach her eyes. A chill ran up Arya's spine, but Finnigan's warmth beside her was comforting. It reminded her that whatever happened, she wasn't in this alone.

"Good morning, Fraeya." The Elven "Queen" stood from her throne and walked down the golden embellished stairs to the main floor of the large ballroom.

The ceiling in here was so high, Arya doubted that even a Giant could reach up to touch it. Several glittering crystalline chandeliers hung from the elevated ceiling, casting rainbows on every surface of the room. Arya took notice of the twisted expression on Finnigan's face. He was in anguish. Unable to reach out and touch so many shiny things. She grabbed his hand and gave it a squeeze, pulling him back down to earth.

"Good morning, Mother." Arya forced the last word out of her mouth. She wasn't a liar; she took great pride in telling the truth. But she supposed that standing in the wake of this deceitful woman, she had no choice but to lie for her own safety. If she gave any indication she knew Lorelei was being less than truthful, they'd throw her off of the island without a moment's hesitation. Or worse.

"I'd like to give you a tour of the grounds. Your Leprechaun friend can come along. And then, you have a day of preparation for the ball."

"I thought this was what I'm going to wear tonight." Arya held up the fabric of her skirt, looking down at the spectacular garment.

"Oh no, darling. Look at you. That's a day dress. You need an evening gown for an event this important." The Elven Queen stepped closer to Arya and cupped the girl's jaw with her long fingers. She pouted her perfect lips. "We'll teach you. Don't worry."

When Lorelei let go of her, Arya could still feel the imprint of the cold fingers against her skin. Lorelei looped an arm through Arya's and walked through the large doorway that led out of the ballroom to the royal gardens. Even surrounded by the towering castle walls, the sanctuary was still teeming with life, full of herbs and flowers and fresh fruit. It was a *paradise*. The sound of waves crashing against the shore and the smell of salt water were still noticeable from here, but not as much as they had been from the outside of the massive fortress.

"This is where we grow all of the vegetables, flowers, fruits, and herbs on the island. Our district of the kingdom is completely self-reliant. The only trading we do is with the Wood Elves on occasion, the Glowyr, and the Goblins of Blackrock. Couldn't have Elves in those dirty mines, even if it does build a place this beautiful." Lorelei scrunched her nose at the idea of it. "I'll teach you how to run the castle from here."

"O-of course. Running the castle…"

"Don't be scared, darling. It's a big task, that's no lie, but in time, you'll know everything you need to know. You're like me. I can tell that already. Clever. Beautiful. You know how to use what you have to get what you want."

"But I don't—"

"Don't interrupt." Lorelei stopped walking for a moment, and then continued. "I can give you anything in the whole world, my darling. Say the word and it's yours."

"I…" Arya blinked a few times, and for the first time since her Magyk had begun to flux, Arya *felt* a change. A small one. She could feel her eyes change color and then shift back to the signature turquoise of the High Elves. Lorelei didn't seem to notice, thankfully, so Arya continued talking. "I don't know if this is where I belong…"

"Of course you do." Lorelei spoke softly, standing in front of Arya and taking each of her hands in her own. "We've been waiting here for you all along, waiting for you to come home. Those Mortals that stole you away will never find you here. I'll keep you safe; all of the High Elves will. We protect our own."

Lorelei looked up to one of the second floor windows that over-looked the courtyard.

When Arya followed her temporary mother's line of sight, she found Daenys standing behind the crystalline glass, looking out at them for a moment before he walked away.

"Even if they're only half."

The rest of the tour was a lot easier for Arya. Finnigan walked behind the Elven Queen and the false princess, making a few comments every once in a while about how beautiful the castle was. Then, once they had seen every inch of the glittering palace, the queen escorted Arya back to her room to be prepared once again for the ball.

Luckily, this session with the Halflings wasn't as brutal as the previous one had been. There wasn't any deep scrubbing or pruning or plucking. She already had the basic structure of a princess; she just needed a little embellishing. Her hair was taken out of the braids, left to hang in waves that reminded her of the sea. Now the brain-pulling made sense.

The Halflings did end up putting in a few more braids, but they were looser and only used to pull the hair out of the front of Arya's face and frame the gorgeous tiara she had been given to wear for the evening. Her fingernails were painted every color of the rainbow, blended into a beautiful layer of vivid colors. They painted her face and used the iridescent powder of ground seashells to highlight and emphasize her more Elven features.

Just before they finished, Arya felt a painful pang twisting in her temple, a pain she was almost used to by this point. A drop of silver and gold blood dripped from her nostril. She wiped it away as quickly as she could, while the three Halflings that were making her presentable were distracted mixing colors to rub on her eyelids. When they looked up, the blood was gone, but Arya's eyes were now an unmistakable shade of forest green instead of the translucent turquoise they were supposed to be.

The Halflings didn't acknowledge the change, but they had *definitely* noticed it. Arya knew that *they* knew that she wasn't a High Elf like the queen was trying to convince them. Arya was still very much in flux, and that made her a risk to their safety. After all, if they let the "Queen's" plan slip, they'd certainly be punished.

So, the Halflings continued in fake ignorance, getting the "princess" ready while making idle small talk to pass the time. Once she was finally finished, there was a knock at the door. An attendant was waiting to escort her to the grand staircase that led down into the ballroom.

Arya's golden slippers padded quietly against the marble floors until they reached the landing at the top of the stairs. Finnigan was standing at the bottom, dressed in a suit that complimented her new ball gown perfectly.

The new dress in question was made of golden silken fabric that flowed with every movement. Beautiful crystals were sewn into swirling patterns on her hips and abdomen, and a rainbow shone in the iridescent fabric of her skirt.

So many sparkles had been rubbed into her skin, she thought they might never wash out. The effects of this place would stick with her for a while, she feared.

Finnigan took her arm. His suit was soft to the touch, silky and smooth like the dress she was wearing. The Leprechaun didn't have a crown sitting in his artificially fiery hair, but he was wearing a new ring around his finger. It was gold with a white gem, and as soon as he made contact with her, that familiar pinching pain tore through Arya's temple.

"Ye alright, princess?" Finnigan asked softly.

Arya shook her head. It was like the first time, when Henry gave her the very necklace that was still hanging around her neck.

"We have to get out there." Finnigan looked her over.

She nodded. The pain subsided, so she slowly straightened up.

Before setting foot in the ballroom filled with High Elves, Arya didn't know what it felt like to have all of the eyes in a room on her. She was just a girl from River's End, not the most beautiful or sought-after. Now that she was here, though, even if it was just for tonight, she got the chance to be a princess.

"Elves of the Isle of Highland," Queen Lorelei spoke, breaking Arya from her reverie.

There was some whispering amongst the crowd, awed mutterings and shocked looks. Finnigan glanced at her every few seconds to make sure she hadn't sprouted horns. So far, so good.

"It is my great honor to present to you Princess Fraeya, the long-lost heir to our throne."

The crowd applauded, shouting their support as Arya and Finnigan entered the main floor. A group of musicians stood in the corner of the room with their instruments, and once they received the signal from Lorelei, they started playing.

Arya and Finnigan glided across the floor in time with the music. Slowly, more and more pairs of dancers flooded the floor and they were finally able to slip out unnoticed. They couldn't leave the room quite yet, though. Not while people were waiting in the wings to introduce themselves to the pair.

Daenys was lingering near the doorway. He knew his mother wouldn't suspect anything. Orris was still mingling with the High Elves, after all, and it was no secret that her eldest half-Wood Elf son didn't particularly fit in among either of the races he belonged to. Daenys caught Arya's eyes while she and Finnigan were talking with one of the ladies of the High Court. He flicked his mismatched irises behind him towards one of the servant passages and Arya nodded discreetly.

Upon receiving the signal from Daenys, Arya gave Finnigan's hand a squeeze. Maybe it was the nerves or the exhaustion or the stress eating away at her that caused her eyes to turn green, but whatever it was, the "Queen" and the others around Arya noticed.

And Lorelei was not happy.

"Fraeya?" she asked, her voice soft, but intense. "Look at me."

Arya turned her head and the fake concern in Lorelei's gaze faded to something unreadable, a blank face as she thought, and then anger.

"Imposter! You're not the princess! You're just a Wood Elf in disguise!" The queen shouted, pointing one of her slender, well-manicured fingers at Arya, effectively covering her tracks and her involvement in the matter.

Arya's green eyes widened, as did Finnigan's. The Leprechaun was frozen in place, unsure of what to do for fear of only making things worse. He needed to get Arya to the boat, but how?

"Seize them! Thieves! Liars!" The Queen ordered.

The Elven guards rushed past the frazzled party guests to grab Finnigan and Arya, but Arya's eyes became coated in a smooth inky black and her irises glowed red. The blonde flowed out of her hair, replaced by her natural brown. She grabbed Finnigan's hand and pulled him down the servant passage after Daenys, who had gone in only moments before.

As soon as she could, the false princess ditched her crown and shoes. She found it much easier to run without her dainty slippers, which slid much too easily against the marble floors.

"Well, that went about as well as I expected it to." Daenys muttered, tugging open a door near the kitchens and ushering

Arya and Finnigan inside. "Orris is going to try to buy us some time, but I'm not sure how much. This way."

Daenys pushed a hanging Elven crest out of the way and ducked into the small passage hidden behind it. It was dimly lit there and smelled heavily of fish, the tunnel barely big enough for two of them to stand beside each other. This was the hall used to transport the barrels filled with salmon and perch and whatever else the Halflings managed to catch to the kitchens.

Finally, they reached a large gate in front of which sat a boat loaded with all of their gear and the few Halflings Daenys could manage to gather on such short notice.

"Arya and Finnigan, meet Moss, Fauna, and Soora, some of my mother's favorite Halflings."

Finnigan let go of Arya's hand and walked over to Daenys, who was standing next to the chain on the wall that would raise the heavy metal gate so they could escape the stupid, shiny place. Moss, a tall green-haired boy with a long, pointed nose and long, pointed ears, helped the others with the chain, and slowly, the gate went up, opening the tunnel to the waters that surrounded the castle.

As soon as the gate was open, the boat started to drift forward. Moss tossed Finnigan an oar and then they both hopped into the wooden craft with Daenys behind them, giving the boat a good push before hopping in himself. They only had to get to shore, which they could see from there, illuminated by the Wood Elves' torches.

The boys rowed as fast as they could while Arya pulled on her brown leather boots, which had been thoroughly cleaned since the last time she'd seen them. As soon as they landed, she was going to get out of her dress and back into her armor. Then, maybe she'd be able to breathe again.

Daenys watched Moss and Finnigan row for a few seconds before lowering his hand into the water behind the boat and kicking up a current of his own. The boat cruised along much faster with Daenys' magic. Arya looked to him for an explanation, but only got a smirk in response. She was grateful, of course. Especially when the whirring of a High Elven arrow zipped past her ear and she and the others ducked into the small wooden boat for cover.

After a few minutes of rowing, the group finally hit the shore. The torches of the Elven boats that were following them across the waters shone bright in the dark night, and the occasional arrow arched into the sand surrounding them. As soon as they gathered their things, they made a run for it, into the safety of the Wood Elves' fortress. It was hard to make out the shape of branches or trees in the woods, but eventually they found the towering mound of burning tree limbs as well as the outstretched branches at the center of the stone refuge.

As expected, Elion was waiting for them inside, his guards armed and ready to protect the Halflings-turned-refugees, fleeing yet another home of theirs. Moss stood in front of Fauna and Soora, ready to defend them from their pursuers if need be. Though the Wood Elves all stood at attention, the High Elves never reached the shore, their boats hovering menacingly in the waters just beyond the territorial line.

There were a lot of things Lorelei was willing to do to protect her secrets. However, starting another civil war with her ex-husband wasn't one of them. Wary eyes watched as all of the golden boats turned around and left the mainland. Daenys exhaled a breath. Someday, he'd have to face his mother for turning her in, but today was not that day.

"That's it?" Arya asked, watching the shiny boats retreat to their lofty castle. She was breathing heavily, leaning against Finnigan for support. The corset she was trapped in had reduced her air capacity tremendously, and if she wasn't careful, she was sure she'd pass out.

"My mother may not have the soundest plans, but she wouldn't start a war over something this miniscule." Daenys sat down on a thick log, resting his head in his hands. "That's assuming she doesn't know about the other escapees."

"She'll never find out. Not until it's too late." Elion smiled proudly, looking down at his son. He then turned to Arya. "A friend came to help while you were away. She's sleeping now, but she'll be ready to depart with you in the morning. In the meantime, I suggest you get some rest. I'm sure you need it after whatever Lorelei put you through."

"Thank ye." Finnigan bowed before taking Arya's elbow and following one of the Wood Elves to the little cabin furnished for guests. He helped her out of her dress, exhausted fingers working to loosen the strings on her corset until she could finally breathe again, and then she changed into a flowing cotton dress to sleep in.

Arya just about collapsed onto the soft mattress beside Finnigan's and let her eyes close, barely able to mumble out a "goodnight" before surrendering to the place between asleep and awake.

Finnigan let out a breath, looking her over before crawling under the thick woven blankets and finally laying down after a long day. He watched Arya's form move, breaths entering and leaving her slowly until he felt safe enough to close his own eyes. *"Goodnight, princess…"*

Chapter 12
NEVER TRUST A FRYNGE WYTCH

Far away from the Elven Lands, all the way on the other side of the Veil, in the sleepy little village of River's End, Henry Smith discovered very quickly that he had yet another problem:

The Mortals of River's End were not stupid.

Actually, they were very clever. They figured out the day after Arya had gone missing that she had run away and they knew Henry must have *something* to do with it. He was able to avoid questioning, mostly, but this was due to the fact that Arya had gone missing on the same night that Finnigan had. With her blue eyes and the circumstances surrounding them, it only made sense that she'd followed the escaped Magykfolk into the Veil, and thus, she was out of the Mortals' reach.

Henry was worried about her. He truly was. He hadn't heard *anything* from her since she'd left. She hadn't even sent him a note by Raven, which he had been hoping for, but realized it could be easily intercepted by anyone in their village who was good with the birds. He had gotten a few premonitions, though: sudden spikes of panic, the feeling of creeping crawly legs up his arm or a sudden racing heart and unexplainable heat flashes.

She was in trouble; he could feel it. Henry knew he'd have to do something about it, and soon.

Henry spent most of his evenings these days watching the sunset. He was there on the hill outside River's End where it all began, where he asked Arya to adventure with him when he should have told her how much he loved her. And he *did* love her, there was no question about it, but he had been so set on leaving their twisted town, on finding something new and exciting with her at his side. He thought he would have more time with her to figure it all out together.

He had been wrong.

Henry tried to keep a level head, but he was starting to worry that she'd never come back. And he *knew* he shouldn't do that. It was bad for him to think about things like that, to think that he would never see her again. Yet, he couldn't help it. Arya was the only person in his dull village that actually made him happy, the only person that made his colorless life worth living.

So, a few nights later, when Henry had a nightmare about Arya running through the woods, a golden ballgown trailing behind her fair figure, he was a bit startled. She barely looked like herself. There was so much powder and paint caked on her face; he had almost not recognized her. Her hair was platinum blonde at the ends and her eyes were so vivid and green, her ears were pointed like an Elf's, and even her skin seemed to glimmer.

She was running from someone, lights in the distance, the flickering flames of torches and whirring arrows zipping past. Someone was coming for her.

Out of all of his delusional premonitions, all of the thoughts and fears bouncing against the walls of his brain, the nightmares his frantic mind had conjured, this one finally felt *real*. Vividly real. It struck his soul differently, dread sinking deep into his spirit.

Henry didn't wait a single second longer before bursting out of his bed, sweat matting his thick hair to his forehead. He changed his clothes, pulling on a pair of trousers and lacing up his boots as quickly as his shaking fingers would allow. Looking around his room, he hastily shoved some helpful things into his leather satchel: one of his hand-drawn maps, a brass compass, a pouch for water, a small bag of coins. And then, hardly thinking anything of it, Henry hooked a leg over his windowsill and slid the window shut behind him.

He watched the last of the orange hues dip beneath the horizon, slowly fading from sight as the sky went dark. That evening was the first clear one all week; he could count the stars. And so he did, silently begging Asteria to protect him from whatever he was about to do.

The people of the village of River's End had warned their young of the Wytches of the Frynge for all of Henry's life. The Mortals had been tricked by them once before, given a false prophecy that a Mortal would take the throne of Recensere, and so, they'd tried to, starting the Mortal Rebellion as a consequence. In the end, the Rebellion only led to the banishment of the Mortals to the bleak and barren Borderlands.

Henry knew what the Wytches were capable of, but he also knew that even if it seemed like their promises were lies, they always came true in the end. You had to be specific when bargaining with them, or they would twist your wishes against you. He had one chance to get it right.

He crept silently along the side of his house until he reached the Blacksmith workshop. His father's favorite sword was mounted on the wall above a chest full of other weapons. It gleamed, the moonlight reflecting in its perfectly polished blade. He couldn't. If he so much as got a fingerprint on it, he'd be disowned. But after rummaging through the chest and finding next to nothing he knew how to use, he sighed, eyes drawn back up to James Smith's pride and joy.

Well, it *was* for Arya...

So, once he'd dressed himself in the finest leather armor he could find, he gently took down the sword.

It was fine steel, decorated with whatever shiny brown gem the blacksmith had been lucky enough to find. The piece was sharpened to perfection and weighted with absolute balance. He gave it a few practice swings and then sheathed it in its case before hooking it to his belt.

Just before he set out down the path and left the village for the first time in his life, he was stopped by someone.

"Henry, is that you?" It was a kind womanly voice, too old to be Arya coming back for him, but not his mother's voice either.

"Mrs. Miller?" he asked.

She came closer to his lantern and sure enough, it was Arya's mother, a grief-stricken look on her face. Henry's expression softened at the sight of her. He hadn't even considered that Arya's absence would take a toll on Katherine in the same way it was hurting him.

Even if she wasn't Arya's true mother, she was still the woman who had raised her. She had to miss her too.

"Henry, where are you going?" she asked.

"To find Arya." He left out, conveniently, the part about going to bargain with a Frynge Wytch with whatever gold he had managed to find hidden away in the Smiths' house. That was only a stepping stone in his overall goal, after all. Details didn't matter, so long as he found her.

"I knew you would eventually," she stated. There wasn't any anger in her voice. Only sadness, compassion, maybe a touch of guilt. "Listen. Whatever John and James and everyone else in the village said to you, I don't care about why she left. I don't care where she is. I just need you to bring her home. I..." Katherine's eyes filled with tears.

Henry set down his lantern and took the woman into his strong arms, rubbing her back soothingly, as he had done for Arya so many times before. "I'm going to find her. I promise."

"Bring her home, Henry." Katherine whispered, grasping onto the blacksmith's son. "Please. I have to tell her I'm sorry. For all of this..."

"I will."

Katherine finally let go of him and he picked his lantern off of the ground. Just as he turned to walk away, she took hold of Henry's wrist and pressed a small white gem into his hand. It reminded him of the gemstone on the necklace he had given Arya. It tingled with power, resting in his palm with an energy he had only felt when Arya was in his arms.

Magyk.

"Give this to the Frynge Wytches. They'll do anything you want." Katherine had something new in her voice, determination or something similar to it. How she had known about his little trip to visit the Wycked Magyk casters was a mystery to him.

"How do you—"

"How else are you going to get through the Veil?"

Henry only nodded. Katherine knew better than most that the only way the Mortal boy in front of her was going to get past the Magykal border keeping him out was to make a bargain with one of them.

He thanked Katherine for the little token of Magyk that would hopefully help him find his best friend and then he traveled down the beaten path, off into the Frynge.

●●◐○○○◐◑●●

By sunrise, he had come across the first cottage. They were spread out in this barren place, each Wytch's home settled further and further than the last. It was even more bleak and hopeless than the Borderlands, the little homes spread out so far, he could hardly see the next one on the horizon.

The only reason Henry could tell the sun had risen at all was because it was getting lighter outside despite the thick clouds in the sky. Out in the Frynge, it always looked like a storm was coming, and yet it never did. The angry hue of the sky sent shivers through his body. This was not a good place.

All of the grass was dead, and the trees grew nothing but branches, gnarled and absolutely Wycked. Instead of leaves clinging to the sides of their houses, the buildings in the Frynge were covered only in twisted vines dominated by long thorns.

Henry walked up to the craggy wooden door with the cracked window and took a deep breath, swallowing thickly. Just as he was raising his trembling hand to use the old brass bat-shaped knocker, the door swung open abruptly, causing his heart to race and his stomach to drop.

"Henry Smith. I've been waiting for you," called a worn old voice. Unpleasant chills ran through him and he froze in place. "Well come on in, boy. Don't be shy. I don't eat children...*anymore.*" A gnarled laugh followed that statement. When he still didn't reply or come through the door, she called again. "I'm only kidding, dear one. Don't get your trousers in a knot."

Henry gulped and stepped over the threshold into the cottage, which was much cozier than he'd expected. There weren't any decapitated Mortal heads hanging from the ceiling or jars full of fingers, like he had been warned. Instead, there was a roaring fireplace, a nice knitted rug, and about a million candles flickering, filling the warm space with soothing light.

In the corner of the room, there was the Wytch standing over her cauldron. It didn't smell like anything devious. In fact, it smelled like stew. Or soup. There wasn't any oddly colored fog surrounding it or glowing Magyk or anything that was off-putting.

"I'm just about finished making stew, if you'd like some." She flicked her wrist and a wooden bowl and spoon floated into his hands. Henry stood there in shock. He was expecting a monster, and all he had gotten was this kindly old woman.

"Um, sure." He was too polite to reject her offer, but he didn't intend on eating it.

She beckoned him closer with her finger and then ladled some stew into his bowl before ladling some into her own.

"I hope you like cream and potatoes."

"I'm used to it."

"Not the way I make it." She held up a little jar of spices that he had heard of, but had never tasted. The Mortals grew some herbs and such back in his village, but they didn't have access to *these*. The precious spices were from the Sands of Waye, and since the Wytches and Mortals had been cut off from the rest of the kingdom, they were very hard to come by. "Simple duplication spells have helped my spice collection survive through my last few decades of banishment. Take a seat, Henry. We have much to talk about."

Henry's eyes narrowed and he studied the short, wrinkled lady. A knitted shawl was draped over her hunched shoulders, and a few gleaming rings adorned her thin, crooked fingers. "How do you know my name?"

"I saw you coming months ago. I've just been waiting for you to finally work up the courage to venture all the way out here. All it took was the Magyk girl slipping beyond the Veil, eh?"

"I was hoping you could help me get inside the Veil, too. So I can go find her."

"Well, there's a lot more land inside there than I think you're accounting for, boy. You can't just go in blind; you need some way to locate her," the Wytch pointed out.

Henry nodded. "That's true, but how do I get past the barrier to begin with?"

"We'll handle that after we get you headed in the right direction. Finding her is more important than being able to get past that blasted border." She took a large spoon of stew to her lips, blew on it until the steam was gone, and then ate it. "Let's finish our stew and then get to work. The day is young."

Henry listened, stirring around his stew, but still too untrusting to eat any. Soon, the Wytch was finished with hers and walked over to a workstation tucked into the corner of the room.

MORGAN M. STEELE

A few large leather books sat on the wooden surface, and even more candles lit the space. She turned the pages of one of the books and then held out her hand, spindly fingers inviting an offering. Henry looked at her quizzically until she said, "The compass, clever boy."

Nodding, he rummaged through his satchel to find it, handing her the brass trinket. And then, remembering it was there, he handed over the white stone as well, figuring he'd have to give it to her at some point anyway.

The Wytch let out a long hum, her thumb rubbing the smooth surface of the rare gem. "It's been a while since I've come in contact with a Shifter Stone. Very valuable, these. Powerful. It'll get the job done and still have Magyk left to spare. Tell me, do you have anything that belonged to her? A hair, a shoe, anything? Even a lucky coin or a ribbon from her dress would work."

Henry thought for a long while. Did he have anything of Arya's? Had she given him anything that he had with him? Anything at all?

"Not that I can think of. Not *with* me, at least…"

"Not even a…memory?" Her voice was expectant.

Henry furrowed his brows. He wasn't sure how a memory would work to accomplish their goal, but this woman *did* have Magyk after all. She had the black and green hair and the violet-gray eyes to prove it.

"I have a memory."

"Tell me about the last time you saw her."

"It was…the Harvest Festival. Night had fallen. Kids were laughing in the center of town, wrapping ribbons around the maypole. I took her down to the tunnels and we found out what the Mortals were doing down there, torturing Magykfolk, a particularly feisty Leprechaun, specifically. They used some potion to drain his Magyk, make him bigger. Once they left, we set him

122

free and took him to the Veil. Arya...found out the day before that she was different. I told her to go with him, and she did, and I haven't seen her since."

The Wytch wiggled her nose and focused all of her energy on the boy's chest as it welled up with warm feelings of his beloved. A physical item would have been easier, but she pulled the pieces of emotion from his memories of her. The sunset. Arya's eyes turning blue, and then the next day at the Veil when he had let her go.

It was so powerful, so recent and raw and real that the essence flowed right out of him and into the compass in her hand. The cold metal went warm in her palm and when she looked down at it, the needle spun and spun and spun until it stuck. The Wytch moved it around a little bit, testing her Magyk, and the needle adjusted to point at the same spot, like she had intended. Sure enough, after all of these years, she hadn't lost her touch.

"The compass will take you right to her, wherever she is." The Wytch attached the compass to a long chain, hanging it around his neck before she walked across the cottage to a smaller cauldron. It was only about a fourth of the size of the large one that was sitting in her fireplace, full of stew.

This second cauldron was filled with a translucent liquid that swirled with rainbows and iridescent colors. It smelled like white roses, which Henry realized was because of the small shrub of them sitting in the silver planting pot beside the cauldron.

"It's filled with Hallowyng tears and blessed by the Sacreds. It has prophetic affinities," she explained, "like a looking glass of sorts. It'll show you where she'll be."

"So, where she's going."

"Yes. Where she will be by the time you get out there." The Wytch nodded. She raised her bony hands above the cauldron and spoke a language Henry had never heard. Something ancient. And then, after the archaic mumblings and murmurings, she whispered a name. "*Arya.*"

The liquid swirled and swirled before steam rose from it and a picture became clear in the murky waters. A blizzard. Pine trees covered in snow. Arya was there, but she looked different than she had in his nightmare. This time, she had hair as white as the snow falling all around her and eyes as chilly and fragile as icicles. She was wearing a furry white cape on top of brown leather armor.

With her was a boy Henry recognized as Finnigan, the Leprechaun he and Arya had set free on the night everything changed. He was red-haired again with green eyes, and he stood an inch or two shorter than Arya. The Magyk was wearing off, albeit slowly.

There was another boy Henry didn't recognize, one with thick tufts of green hair and the exaggerated pointed features of a Goblin. He had a glittering Fae hanging lifeless in his arms, frost coating her wings and snow stuck in her blonde hair.

He heard the deep menacing growl of a beast of some kind, maybe a bear or a wolf they were destined to cross paths with.

"*Arya! Stay away from it!*" Finnigan shouted before Henry could. For some reason, watching this scene unfold felt familiar to him. Maybe this had been in one of his nightmares, too, but he didn't remember it aside from the faint feeling tickling the back of his brain. The beast growled again, and then the snippet of future ended.

Henry couldn't shake the feeling of dread that sank deep into his bones. Something horrible was going to happen if he didn't find her *immediately*. Thanks to the Wytch, he knew what was coming, so he could warn her, give her the time she needed to fight or flee from whatever creature was threatening her.

"How do I get to her?" Henry turned to the Wytch, his eyes wide and his body trembling. "There has to be something I can do..."

She thought for a long moment before opening her mouth to speak. "Well, dear boy, that depends...What would you give to find her?"

"Anything," he replied without hesitation, desperation thick in his voice and tears running down his cheeks.

The Wytch's features twisted into a Wycked smile that somehow made the Mortal boy feel even worse.

"Just what I needed to hear..."

Chapter 13
Through Ice and Snow

The next morning, Arya didn't remember where she was until the light was shining through the window of the cabin in the Elven Lands. She was wrapped up in a thick woven blanket, half-expecting to find herself still wearing the glimmering golden ballgown from the Isle of Highland. She'd forgotten Finnigan had helped her change out of her beautiful prison and into something comfier before bed. One thing from the previous night did linger, however; colorful Elven powders and paints were smeared across her face like an abstract painting made by someone who was just trying out colors on the canvas in front of them.

Arya sat up and took a look at her surroundings. She'd passed out so quickly after all of the running for their lives that she hadn't even noticed she and Finnigan had ended up in the same bed. Giggling to herself, she shook her head and ran her fingers through her messy bedhead, catching a flash of color in the corner of her eye.

There was a mirror hanging on the wall in front of them, and in her reflection, Arya noticed that the tips of her hair had gone red. Leprechaun red.

She laughed in disbelief, playing with the colorful strands. After spending so much time with Finnigan, it was inevitable, a matter of time before her Magyk dabbled in his. Her eyes were green too, she noticed, and her ears were pointed, but that could have been leftover Elf that didn't want to leave her just yet.

After a couple of quiet minutes, Finnigan blinked and sat up in the bed he and Arya had unknowingly shared the previous night. He looked at her, a sleepy haze settling over his eyes, which were even greener that morning than they had been since he'd set foot through the Veil. The Leprechaun stretched and yawned before he finally remembered what had happened the night before. The ball. The escape. The Elven Lands.

Around his finger was the gold ring with the white gemstone that the High Elves had given him. He studied all of its details, the leaves carved into its thick band, the way the pearly stone glistened in the sunlight. It was so beautiful. He realized after a few long moments that he had been looking at the shiny trinket for too long, his eyes glued to the glimmering orb in the center of the ring. This meant one thing: the most dangerous of his Leprechaun tendencies was returning to him.

So, instead, he turned his attention to Arya, hiding the ring beneath the blanket.

"Yer lookin' a little red in the hair there, Arya." Finnigan grinned confidently as he stretched out the sore muscles in his back. Every bone in his body ached, a reverse growing pain that came with getting smaller. "Spendin' too much time with the wee folk, I think."

"Yeah, me too." She gave him a playful shove. "We made it, though."

"That, we did." His green gaze lingered on her features. The Leprechaun noticed that his friend had taken on even the smallest details of his kind, like the freckles that were halfway hidden beneath the paint smeared across her cheeks.

"We need to get you out of those clothes and wipe the rainbow off of my face." Arya motioned to the colors that had once been beautiful now marred by sweat trails and sleep. It was quite a mess, but with some cloth and water she found in a jug in the corner of the bedroom, Arya was able to clean it off without too much trouble, only a few stray sparkles left on her bare face.

The necklace Henry had given her so long ago was still hanging around her neck under her nightgown, resting just beneath her collarbones. She smiled sadly when she thought about him. It wasn't all that long ago that she had left her Mortal village for the forests of Recensere, and he already felt so far away. The whole time she had lived with the Mortals felt like a dream since she had crossed through the Veil, fuzzy and faint, the details bleeding together into one cohesive sludge of memories. Now, she was really awake, seeing things for the first time, hearing them, *feeling* them.

Henry Smith was the only thing from River's End that felt real anymore, and if they didn't find the source of Arya's Magyk in time, she'd never get to see him again.

She shook off the dark thoughts and turned to Finnigan. He had a stupid grin on his face.

"What's the matter with you, Finn? Why do you look so happy?"

"Well, it's not every night ye get tae sleep with a princess in yer arms." He quipped, earning another annoyed shove from the girl.

"Shut up. Let's just thank the gods *that* wasn't my home." She'd had enough of Lorelei after one day; she wasn't sure how Daenys put up with her on a regular basis. She shook her head and peered out the window into the rest of the camp.

Already, the Wood Elves were awake and working, even though the sun was just barely up over the horizon. Pink still tickled the edges of the sky, and one of the moons shone white above them, a glaring reminder of the eternally running clock that was ticking down to Arya's impending demise. Time didn't care about her, and neither did the moons.

While she was distracted, Finnigan pulled the map out of Arya's bag and compared it to the list of places they had yet to venture to. Quite a few of them were in the Square, the lively district surrounding Castle Transverto. They would head there after visiting the Blackrock Mines and meeting up with Agathon.

After all, they didn't let just *anyone* into the city the Shifters dwelled in. If they had a Centaur with them, their chances were much better.

Finnigan figured then, by that logic, the only place they *could* go next was the December Woodlands to visit the Wynterborn. And that meant they needed to stock up on furs, and quick. They could take a trip to the marketplace in the Elven camp before heading out. Without some heavier armor, they were sure to freeze solid before they even set foot in the nearest settlement of Wynterborn.

This close to the Wynterlands, there had to be fur dealers they could barter with. There was no way the merchants wouldn't take advantage of the potential travelers coming through these parts.

Finnigan wondered just how much fur they could get for the shiny new ring around his finger...

He was taken aback by the thought that had just run through his head. *Never* while he was in Clover Town was he willing to trade something that valuable for someone other than himself. Never. His little Leprechaun hands were bad at letting go. But here he was, ready to give it up for Arya.

Maybe it wasn't just pieces of him that were rubbing off on her. Maybe there were things he was taking from her, too.

So, while Arya stayed in the cabin to wait for word from Elion or Daenys about the mysterious visitor that had arrived the day before, Finnigan went down to the marketplace. The stalls were all stocked, Elves and Satyrs and other woodland creatures flitting from merchant to merchant while glowing green Sprites buzzed above them.

As it turned out, the little treasure wrapped around his finger was a Shifter Stone, and it was extremely valuable. So valuable, in fact, that Finnigan walked away from the fur dealer with enough fur for the two of them and then some, two pairs of lined boots, and a few pounds of dried meats from the butcher. Even after all of that, the merchants gave him a sack of coins as his change. And that was *one ring* with one *tiny* Shifter Stone embedded into it. He didn't even want to know what Arya's necklace was worth.

So, once he'd finished his shopping, Finnigan returned to the cabin to find that Arya was no longer standing there alone, looking at the moon. Instead, Elion and Daenys had joined her, along with a blonde-haired Fae, her glittering wings facing the door when the Leprechaun walked in. "Faiya?"

"Finn." Arya motioned him to step further inside, and he did, setting the supplies he'd gotten on the bed.

"Your friend here has journeyed a long way to help." Elion motioned to Faiya, who offered a small nod and a shy smile.

"My...mother sent me. She was worried you might need a healer, what with," Faiya's eyes flicked towards Arya, who appeared to be something between a Wood Elf and a Leprechaun at the moment, "the circumstances the way they are."

"It's much appreciated." Arya nodded, trying not to let the grave implications get to her. Her condition was indeed worsening. She could feel the spool inside of her unraveling as the days dragged on, and she wasn't sure how much longer she'd be in a somewhat stable condition.

"Moss is going with you as well." Daenys told them. "His mother lives in Blackrock. He wants to go home."

Arya, someone who more than knew the pain of aching for both a home she knew and a home she didn't, was more than willing to let the Half-Goblin into their ever-growing party. "Then I guess we're taking him home."

Daenys nodded and smiled a small, but grateful smile. He wanted to do more for the Halflings, but Fauna and Soora had both opted to stay in the Elven Lands until they received word from King Valens, telling them what to do and where to go. Getting Moss home was the least he could do after everything Lorelei had put him through, but Daenys promised himself someday he'd make it up to him in a more meaningful way.

"Thank you for everything you've done for us. You've helped more than you know." Elion gave a slight bow and then left the cabin with Daenys in tow, letting Moss in on their way out.

Finnigan was quick to show the others the furs he'd gotten at the market, helping Arya sew some into her cloak, and attach a hood to her otherwise fully-covering armor. Up until this leg of the journey, they'd never had a real need for fostering warmth. Even at night, the southern Recenserean forests were only mildly chilly at worst, definitely not cold enough to warrant furry hoods and reinforced armor. But the enchantment encompassing the Northern Mountain and the forests surrounding it was brutal, and they'd need to bundle up if they didn't want to lose a few fingers and toes to the biting winds.

Once they were all properly dressed for the climates of the December Woodlands, Moss, Faiya, Finnigan, and Arya bid goodbye to the Elven Lands and marched down the path leading to where they would find the den of the Wynterborn.

Arya wore a white furry hood over her head, partially covering her face. Her features were constantly changing, eyes transitioning from green to blue to brown, never freezing in one hue for very long. Just before they stepped through the arch of trees that divided the Elven Lands from the rest of the Recenserean woods, Arya stopped in her tracks.

The girl's eyes were wide, flashing through colors quickly. Her limbs trembled, jolting with the untamed power that was coursing through her veins. Arya's heart buzzed, fingers tingled, lungs *screamed* for air. Silver-gold blood dripped from her nose and she felt a stinging, singeing pain more intense than she had felt since this all began. She dropped to her knees, her vision spotty and head spinning.

Finnigan reached out to touch her, but the white-hot pain flashed through him too. Immediately, he ripped his hand away from her and checked his palm for burn marks, finding only unscathed skin.

Faiya rushed over to Arya next, golden dust drifting behind her fluttering wings. She stood in front of her, assessing the situation as best as she could. This was the reason she had come. She knew Arya and Finnigan couldn't handle these outbursts on their own for much longer. Something was bound to go wrong, and when it did, they would need a healer. A Fae.

"Move. I need space." Faiya told the boys. Once they'd backed up to a safe distance, she focused her Magyk into her right hand and then pressed it against Arya's chest, letting her light latch onto the source of the problem. The raw power zinged through Faiya from her fingertips to her toes, snapping something inside of her, but she held tight, not relenting until her Magyk started to work.

Arya blinked a few times, faltering, and then the flashing stopped. Faiya had stabilized her somehow, soothing the roaring fire in her chest.

"Feeling alright, princess?" Finnigan asked softly, kneeling down beside Arya where she had fallen. He cautiously offered her his hands, half-expecting another jolt of energy to zap him as soon as their skin made contact, but nothing happened. "Here, give me hands a squeeze. I'm right here. Take yer time."

Arya nodded. "Okay…" Her warm hands gripped his larger ones, fingers still shaky and breaths still shallow. She swallowed and looked up at him.

"Can ye stand for me? Do ye want tae try?"

"Y-yeah." She felt a little woozy, but she had been lightly woozy since the moment her eyes turned blue at the river with

Henry. So, slowly, she let him help her up, the feeling trickling back into her legs. "Thanks. I…I think it's alright now. Thank you, Faiya. Whatever you did worked."

"Of course." Faiya nodded, brushing herself off once she'd straightened back up.

The group continued, and though she didn't say it, Faiya now had a pain in *her* head, a faint twisting one that was growing sharper each minute they walked on. Yet, when asked about it, she shook it off, blaming it on the fact that the cold was getting to her. It *was*, sure, but this pain was due to much more than the biting wind and freezing air.

Faiya knew there was something inside her that wasn't supposed to be there.

So, the group marched on through the icy winds that were getting stronger as they ventured further from the Elven Lands and deeper into the December Woodlands, unaware of the secret threat budding just beneath their noses.

After a few miles, snow began to fall, drifting down in heavy flakes the size of coins. Arya had never seen snow like this, so constant and heavy, weighing down the sturdy pine trees and covering the path entirely. It was hard to make out the land ahead of them, so once the sky went dark, the group found the first building they could: what appeared to be an abandoned barn.

When they peered inside, there was nothing and no one, no animals, no bats or owls, only hay and a few stray gusts of snow that had followed them in the open door.

Moss lit the lantern at the entrance of the large barn and Finnigan helped Arya build a little fire inside a circle of stones. The four of them set down their packs and sat down for the first time all day. Arya arched her back and leaned against her arms. Finnigan sat beside her with Moss on his right and Faiya next to Moss.

When the Leprechaun looked at Arya, he found that her hair was now tinged with a hint of white on the ends. Her eyes had settled into an icy blue, and her ears had once again come to a point. She looked like a Wynterborn, Finnigan realized as she untied her furry cape from around her shoulders. She really did. And as the minutes ticked by, the white continued to creep up her hair from the tips, making her look more and more like a child of the snow.

Moss and Faiya watched in awe as the change took place. They had never seen someone's Magyk fluctuating quite as much as Arya's was right now. It was dabbling in something she might be, and it was latching on tighter than it ever had. This could be it.

Maybe she was finally home.

After the group had let the fire warm their freezing limbs, Finnigan spoke up. "I'll take first watch."

"No, I've got it." Faiya shook her head. Although her headache was slowly worsening, she knew it wouldn't go away with sleep. In fact, she felt like closing her eyes, even if only for a bit, might make it worse. "Fae only need a few hours of sleep. Someone can just wake up a little early and I'll rest then."

"If ye insist." Finnigan shrugged. He unpacked some of the dried meats, handing them to Arya and Moss.

Faiya held up her hand, shaking her head as she reached into her own supplies for her enchanted little pouch of berries. "I don't eat meat."

"Neither do I, usually, but this trip has been full of new experiences." Finn chuckled, digging in.

"All of this snow reminds me of the Wynter Festival." Moss sighed, a smile on his face. "Lorelei always made us haul in the *biggest* tree and cover it in ribbons. I haven't had a proper one in so long…" He shook his head. "My mother used to spend so long knitting presents for all of the miners. I'd help her bake the *best* pies and then all of the Goblins and Glowyr would come together…"

"The Fae all have a healing circle. We join hands around our tree, sing songs, rejuvenate the life force in the Glade. It's my favorite time of year."

"In Clover Town, we give each other gifts and have a big feast. Last year, I got me Mam a bracelet." Finnigan took a sip of water and turned to Arya. "What about ye? What do ye do in River's End?"

"We don't have Wynter Festival," Arya admitted quietly. "I've heard of it, but…a lot of our holidays went away when the Mortals were banished."

"You don't have Wynter Festival?" Moss asked, his excited expression falling. "Oh, I'm sorry. That…that's really sad."

"The only thing we celebrate is the Harvest. We don't have any flowers, so we don't have a Flower Festival. We…things are different out there. Very, very different." Arya stared at her hands before looking up at Moss and Faiya and Finnigan. "I really, really like it here. I was so blind, you know? I was used to what I had and I thought I never wanted anything else, but now that I'm here, I would *never* go back."

"For what it's worth, we're glad tae have ye." Finn reached over and rested his hand on top of hers. "Yer one of us, Arya. This is where ye belong."

Arya smiled softly, nodding, her fingers intertwining with Finnigan's.

The four chatted a little while longer around the crackling fire before finally settling down for the night. Once again, Arya found herself in Finnigan's arms, not that she minded. He was warm and he kept *her* warm, so she let him hold her as she listened to his heart beat inside his chest. Soon, he would be too small to do this, to hold her; she had to make these moments last.

Faiya watched Arya curl into Finnigan and sighed. The girl with the white hair, though she was making the most of a bad situation, was falling apart inside. She knew Arya needed someone like her. Maybe that was what had caused Faiya to run away from the Glade and not look back.

Getting permission from Faedella wasn't guaranteed, so Faiya hadn't asked for it, she simply flew to the Elven Lands, hoping for the best. She knew their journey wouldn't be easy. In fact, it would get rather dangerous once the group traveled to some of the farther regions, but with Arya's only source of dependable protection getting smaller and smaller by the day, they needed someone she could count on.

What would Faiya's mother think if she knew where her only daughter had run off to? She probably wouldn't be happy. Additionally, what would she think if she knew that Faiya had something volatile inside her? That would only make her mother's fears worse. Though she hadn't meant for it to happen, a piece of the changing girl had found a home inside Faiya, and it did *not* like its new host.

The pain in Faiya's head got worse as the hours ticked on, leaving her hazy and frazzled in the quiet barn, which was silent aside from the sounds of the fire crackling and Moss' snoring.

Soon enough, Moss woke up, stretching his long limbs and looking to the glittering Fae who was sporting an odd glow in the firelight. However, the Half-Goblin was too tired to notice something was off.

"Get some sleep, Faiya." He yawned as he spoke, leaning himself against a bale of hay. "You look like you need it more than I do."

"I'm okay." She shook her head. "Fae stay up through the night to use the moons' Magyk. I can make it."

"We're inside. There's no moon Magyk here. Get some rest." He tilted his head, giving her fair warning that he was just as stubborn, if not more so, than she was.

The Fae huffed before laying down in her thick sleeping roll. Finnigan had done them a favor by lining their new sleeping rolls with fur. It made for a toasty resting place that kept her wings warm. Moss sighed, looking at the others. Faiya hadn't changed at all on the outside, but now that he was more awake, there was something about her that was odd. Off. He could feel it. His keen Goblin senses put him on the right track. Something was out of place, he just didn't know what.

Then, there was the matter of the ever-shrinking Leprechaun. When Moss talked to Daenys in the Elven castle, the Elf prince had told Moss about what had happened to Finnigan, what the Mortals did to him. Though he should have been terrified of the abilities the Mortals had, he wasn't. He felt the opposite, in fact. The Half-Goblin felt guilty about the hope it filled him with. Goblins, as all the folk of Recensere knew, were not much known for their good looks. As if being a Halfling didn't already hinder his chances at finding someone to love him, his bold nose and green hair certainly did not help matters.

Maybe there was a way the Mortals could make him human, too, even if it wasn't meant to last.

Arya didn't mean to, she wasn't sure how it had happened, but somehow, the green-haired boy's thoughts became a murmur within her own. She blinked a few times, adjusting her position in her shared sleeping roll with Finnigan. Perhaps she had dreamed it? No, it didn't seem so. Something about their proximity to the Wynterborn was affecting her in unseen ways, it seemed.

"I think you're handsome, Moss," she whispered, snuggling deeper into Finnigan's chest.

"What?" Moss chuckled softly, his eyes settled on her.

Arya's light blue eyes were no more than little glowing slits in the flickering fire light. She blinked them a few times before continuing, "Don't worry so much about changing. Believe me, it's not all it's cracked up to be."

"Not everyone is so accepting..." Moss thought about how the Goblins had been shut away in the mines with the Glowyr, away from all of the other people of the kingdom. How the Halflings had been rejected. He was not one, but two things no one wanted: Goblin and Mortal.

"Well, there are people who are. Those are the people who matter. The rest of them...don't know what they're talking about." Arya's voice was a little louder now, but still quiet enough to not wake her sleeping companions. "And besides, something about you...you look like someone I know back home. Someone *very* handsome."

Moss waited for more words of wisdom from the sleepy changing girl, or even clarification about this handsome stranger she claimed he looked like, but none came. She had dozed off again, leaving Moss with an odd, fuzzy feeling welling up in his chest. Some of the first words the girl had spoken to him had been these words of kindness, and he couldn't have been more grateful for it.

If someone like Arya, who seemed to belong *everywhere*, could accept him for who he was, maybe...just maybe, he could too, in time.

Chapter 14

THE WYNTERBEAST

The group awoke the next morning rested enough, but sore from sleeping on the ground. Their fur-lined sleeping rolls had kept out the cold, but they couldn't keep out the lumps in the earth beneath them.

Finnigan and Moss used a bucket of snow to put out the remaining embers of the fire from the night before. Lonely wisps of smoke swirled up into the lofty old barn, and the group donned their furry cloaks and heavy packs of supplies once more.

"Good morning, princess." Finnigan was wearing that confident grin again as he stretched and yawned and looked at Arya, whose hair was now entirely white aside from a tiny bit of brown clinging to her roots and a slight red tint creeping up the bleached ends.

"Good morning...Finnigan?" Arya stood beside him and noticed something that caused her eyebrows to furrow. He was a solid two inches shorter than her. He had to look up to her when she was standing close enough. "Looking a little...*little* there, Finn."

"Gettin' back to me wee size, it seems." He looked down at his ever-shrinking body with a mix of relief and sadness. If he got any smaller, Arya would have to carry him from place to place so he could keep up with the others. With a fake smile, he chuckled and said, "It's about time."

"Yeah." Arya faked a laugh too, the hint of red flowing out of her white locks and the tinge of green leaving her icy blue eyes.

When Arya brushed against Finnigan, she was cold to the touch. She looked less human than she ever had, but there was still a hint of Mortal in her blood. Though, when they got closer to the Wynterborn, he wondered if that would change.

"Let's get a move on." The glittering Fae was already in motion, packing away her things and bundling up to face the cold winds that raged just outside the barn's wooden doors. Her wings twitched a little bit, but the other three didn't notice. She seemed normal. Distant, like she had been since they settled down for the night, but it wasn't concerning enough to warrant their attention.

Moss nodded and started to pack, tugging on his thick fur coat and lacing up his heavy boots. The knitted hat on his head didn't cover his long ears, but it was good enough, he decided. At least it covered up his thick tufts of green hair, a dead giveaway of his Halfling status. Instead of having greenish skin like the rest of the Goblins, Moss had gotten green hair somehow, the feature for which his parents had named him. Maybe it was just a cruel trick of the fates, making him stand out even more than he already did.

Finnigan opened the door once he saw that everyone was ready and led the group into the icy winds.

The December Woodlands were colder than any Mortal winter that had ever graced the Borderlands. Arya had seen snow before, but to travel through a place that was *always* cold and covered in feet of white fluff while icy winds howled across the gaps between the trees, was something entirely different. This eternal blizzard was hazardous, and the further they trekked, the more dangerous it became.

There were worn old signs standing beside the paths that ran through the thick trees. They were wooden, carved with symbols Arya felt like she recognized, but she had to get close and scrape the ice off of them to even attempt to read the directions to the settlement of Wynterborn they had to find.

It was no easy feat.

Many times, the group ended up following the wrong fork in the road and had to trek back to the previous sign and try again. Faiya tried to help the white-haired girl decipher the runes, but her Wynter Rune reading skills were rusty at best. She mostly ended up squinting at them until the pain in her head picked back up and she had to stop, offering some sliver of translation to the others before going silent again.

So, forward and backwards they went, chasing dead ends and following false paths with no chance of finding where they needed to be until the sky started to darken and the stars began to emerge from their hiding places once again, arranging themselves in the glimmering constellations that lit the night.

Flashing rainbow ribbons began to dance across the dark velvet, making Arya's heart flutter as she watched the moving beauty before her. She'd heard tales of these dancing lights as a girl, but never expected them to be so beautiful or colorful. Few people aside from the Wynterborn had ever ventured this far north to see them, and she doubted anyone in her village had paintings or drawings of them from before the Rebellion.

Arya's breath rose before her in puffs of steam, her face concealed by the white fur cloak that was draped around her neck and shoulders. Her feet were so cold she could barely feel her toes, and her fingers had gone numb long ago, even while they were protected inside her new gloves.

It was in that quiet moment, while Arya was admiring the winter night and willing the feeling back into her limbs, that the first disastrous thing happened: Faiya's headache came back with a new fury. She had been fighting it off all day and night, ignoring it in the hopes that it would simply go away, or that her healing tendencies would work inside of her to clear it up naturally. They had not. Instead, it had only grown, festering and growing into something she could not hope to ignore or contain any longer. She blinked a few times, her body jolting with the force of the unstable Magyk that had rooted itself inside her when she first healed the changing girl that stood at her side.

Arya's eyes widened as she tore her icy blue irises away from the dancing lights and focused on Faiya. Golden blood was dripping from the Fae's nose, just as it had dripped from Arya's on several occasions. She knew immediately, beyond a shadow of a doubt, that whatever was happening to Faiya was tied to Arya and her worsening condition.

After a few moments of the Fae trembling beside the Half-Goblin, she collapsed into Moss' waiting arms.

"We have to find somewhere to stop." Arya pressed a hand to Faiya's forehead and felt a flash of white-hot pain, fresh and sharp, almost like it was in her own head instead of the Fae's.

It was as soon as the words had found their way out of her mouth that the second disastrous thing found its turn to strike. In the dark woods, Arya heard a growl, animalistic and deep. And hungry.

"Arya! Stay away from it!" Finnigan shouted. Try as he might, he knew that his diminishing stature was not going to help him protect her. Arya could handle herself better than he could, should he attempt to help her.

Once again, as they had on the Isle of Highland, her eyes inked over and flashed red before returning to an icy blue. She stared out into the night, her eyes finally locking on the beast. Its eyes were glowing and golden, sharp in the dark and a contrast to the shadows that surrounded them. Thick brown fur covered it from the tips of its pointed ears to the end of its powerful tail. Large paws stood on the snow-covered ground in a stance of attack. At any moment, it would pounce, plunging its long fangs into her throat.

Arya's heart was thumping in her chest so powerfully she feared it would push past her ribs and escape. Finnigan closed his eyes and said a silent prayer to whichever gods hadn't abandoned him yet that maybe they could give him just a little bit more of his Leprechaun luck back.

But even luck couldn't save them now.

The beast pounced at Finn. Arya shoved the Leprechaun out of the way and took the full brunt of the force. It knocked her through the snow and into a tree. She reeled, holding her head as she tried to get her bearings back. Dizziness swept through her, laced thick with adrenaline. It made the Magyk in her blood boil. She clenched her fists, the knuckles of her fingers going white.

It crept closer, licking its chops and eyeing her like she was dinner. If she didn't figure something out, she might be.

Arya felt Magyk inside her, bubbling and coming to a boil. It was a flavor of power she hadn't felt yet, but it was there, ready to aid her, or so she hoped.

From his spot hiding behind a tree, Finnigan watched in horror as Arya's eyes flashed golden, identical to the eyes of whatever beast was before her. It was the same thing that happened when they'd been kidnapped by the Spyders. Her Magyk was dabbling, and if it stuck, he'd have no way to bring her back.

The golden-eyed girl took a few tentative steps towards the creature. Aside from her eyes, nothing else had changed. Not even her hair, which was still white with the thinnest line of brown at the base of her roots. As she moved, her steps became more confident. Deep in her throat, a growl was welling larger and larger until she couldn't hold it in anymore. She roared so loud the trees shook.

The beast blinked a few times before roaring even louder than the girl. It shook her to her core. Arya's heart raced, but she stood her ground. Fear would only betray her.

"Be careful, Arya," Finnigan whispered.

She hadn't heard him. Nor did she hear Moss or Faiya, which meant hopefully, they had gone to find a safe place far away from this beast.

Another rush overcame Arya. Her eyes reverted back to the icy blue of the Wynterborn and she focused on that feeling: the cold. Pain twisted in her head and silver blood dripped from her nose, but she ignored it, willing the ice into her arms. Frost formed over her fingertips and palms and an icy steam flew off of her hands. She held them in front of her like weapons and prepared herself to strike. Streams of glowing blue energy swirled around her fingers until icicles, long and thick and sharp, took shape. She drew her arm back and hurled them at the creature's face. The first bounced off of it harmlessly and the second missed and exploded against a tree like a chunk of glass shattering into a million pieces.

The attempted attack only made the beast angry. It pounced again, but Arya dodged and it hit the tree behind her. In moments, it was back on its feet once again, eyeing Arya like a piece of food. But this meal was too much work. Now he just wanted her dead.

Arya brought her icy hands together and focused. Her head was spinning and the blood that was leaving her nose was more than a drip, but she had to keep fighting. She had to. She hadn't come this far for nothing. Arya found a sword in her hand made of ice, long and sharp and gleaming in the starlight. It had grown into her tight grip, formed from her fear and the cold welling up inside her.

She swung the sword, charging, but as she struck, the beast knocked it from her hands. Just before he could finish her off, Finnigan made an attempt to tackle the large creature. He didn't get very far, but the distraction gave Arya the opportunity to get back out from under its hold. The beast snarled at Finnigan and pushed him aside with ease. The Leprechaun was light on his feet, and the force of the push sent him flying into a tree. He slumped forward, his head drooping.

Arya was alone now.

The pain in her head was finally enough to force her to her knees, silvery blood running from her nose. Glittering tears slipped down her cheeks and she looked up at her attacker as her Magyk ran dry. The white rushed out of her hair, the blue left her eyes, and for a moment, Arya would have looked Mortal if it weren't for the silver blood trailing down her face.

The beast's large jaw snapped shut, its fangs jutting out from its upper lip, and after a moment of silence, it howled in pain and slumped to the ground. It was bleeding from the side of its chest, thick red blood matting its dark brown fur.

Finnigan was lying knocked out under a tree, the beast was downed, and Arya had no energy left in her body. Every piece of her felt broken, so she just laid down in the snow, listening to the beast's ragged breaths until she could gather the will to move her cold, heavy limbs, staring up at the stars. Her breath fogged up into the air above her and for what felt like an eternity, she was sure she would never get up again.

A few long minutes later, however, Arya scraped herself off of the ground and crawled over to Finnigan. He was bleeding from the back of his head, but it wasn't too serious, just a little blood from the small cut. Still, she wrapped his head in a little scrap of cloth she found in what was left of their scattered supplies.

Next, she made her way over to the beast, which was whimpering softly. There was a mess of its blood soaking into the snow. A feeling of uncertainty washed over her. She wiped the blood from beneath her nose and examined the wounded beast lying in the snow.

She didn't know why she suddenly had the courage to get so close to it. This monster had just tried to kill her. This monster had tried very, *very hard* to kill her, actually. At that point, she should have been scooping up her Leprechaun friend and running, but there was something about the creature that called her to him.

She knelt in the snow and looked at the wound. It was big. She wondered what had done this to him. He hadn't been bleeding before the fight. Maybe she'd been so caught up in the moment, that she hadn't noticed she'd actually struck him after all.

Arya had never taken a life. Never. She had never been hunting with the men of River's End, and when bugs got into her house, she'd always had her father or Henry take it outside. And so, as she looked down at the dying creature, something within her soured. There had to be something she could do.

Her mind wandered to their group's resident healer. Faiya could make it better, but Arya had broken her, too. Why was it that everything she touched seemed to break?

So, the girl knelt there in silence, limbs numb from the cold, head pounding from the fight. The snow was falling slower, now, big flakes catching in the beast's thick brown fur. Its breathing was shallow, inconsistent. She knew that if she did nothing, soon, it wouldn't be breathing at all.

Arya looked to the heavens. Her palms tingled, and a Magyk as warm and small as the flickering flame of a candle lit deep inside of her chest. As the moments ticked on, the power grew, stretching from one tiny candle to a torch the size of her fist. She looked down at her hands, studying the rough skin, and found that very faintly, they were glowing. This Magyk was familiar, and she couldn't pinpoint why until she found herself reaching forward, palms pointed at the beast.

She willed the power swirling around her heart into her hands and it came flowing from the floodgates tucked away inside her. Golden light materialized, warm and swirling, filling the darkness and chasing the shadows into the night.

Arya focused the Magyk, concentrating it into one place and then pushing the healing force from both of her hands onto the large wound. For a few moments, it appeared to do nothing, but then, slowly, the torn flesh began to repair itself. It came together, each side reaching out for the other until finally, they touched. There was a scar in the beast's skin where the gash had been, a patch of white where no fur grew, but he stopped whimpering.

In fact, the creature stopped making noise altogether. The beastly thing stopped moving. Its injured whine became a groan that was almost...human.

It was then that the third disastrous thing occurred.

The beast's large, monstrous form began to retreat into itself. The long, thick brown fur retracted into what appeared to be armor. Huge brown paws thinned into hands, fingers, feet, and toes. His bleary golden eyes looked up at Arya as the healing light continued to flow from her fingertips.

The fur of his face retreated into smooth tan skin, and long tufts of brown hair remained on his now human head. The wolf-like snout shrank into a human nose, fangs becoming teeth—though they were still quite a bit sharper than was considered ordinary—and its claws reverting to fingernails. Hints of extra hair clung to the sides of his face, and his eyes remained golden, but Arya would recognize that face anywhere.

She whispered his name as though if she spoke it, the word might float off into the wintry winds, never to be heard ever again.

"Henry."

Chapter 15

The Boy in the Beast

Henry's golden eyes shone like coins in the moonlit night. They looked up at Arya weakly as the healing Magyk stopped flowing from her fingers. His breaths were labored, heavy, and his shoulders heaved with each one as though he was carrying the weight of the world and it was crushing him. His arms were more defined than Arya remembered, and he had more facial hair now, with thicker eyebrows to match.

"I found you," he whispered, a shaking hand reaching up to tentatively touch her cheek. His head was laying in her lap as tears streamed down her cheeks. Tears of relief, of grief, of guilt. She was the reason he was here. The reason he had...become this thing.

"Henry..." she sobbed, trying to pull him into a more upright position. She couldn't put her feelings into words despite how hard she tried. He was here, and he was different. He had finally followed his dream of crossing the Veil, though she doubted it was in the way he had envisioned it happening.

"You remember what the Mortals said about making deals with Wytches?" Henry groaned as he put some weight on his sore arms. "They were right."

Arya supported him as he shifted his weight so he could pull the girl to his chest, holding her for the first time in too long.

"I could have killed you," Arya sobbed into his shoulder.

He rubbed her back and shushed her. "I could have killed you, too." Henry held Arya tight.

They both sat there for a long time, embracing as they cried, reflecting on everything that had brought them each to that point. Once they'd sat there for a few minutes, enjoying the presence of the other after being separated for so long, the chill of the

December Woodlands got to Arya and she remembered that they were sitting out in the cold.

Arya slowly rose to her feet, with the help of Henry, and began carefully crunching through the snow. Finnigan was still out cold, his breaths rising in front of him as visible puffs every time he exhaled. Arya was just grateful her Leprechaun friend was breathing at all. She knelt down beside him and checked him over for any other injuries. He seemed fine, all things considered, and due to his reduced size, it wasn't hard for her to shift his weight onto herself.

Henry took one of Finnigan's arms and wrapped it around his shoulders, helping Arya carry him. Finn had changed a lot since Henry had seen him last. "He's getting shorter, then. It's wearing off."

"Yeah, it is. Slowly but surely, I guess." Arya shrugged. "We're doing the best we can with it, but I can tell it bothers him sometimes."

"And you haven't run into too much trouble?" Henry knew that this was his best friend he was talking to, but he also knew a lot had changed since he'd last seen her. This was still his Arya, but it was obvious that she wasn't the starry-eyed girl from River's End anymore.

"A little here and there. Fought some Spyders, fled from some High-Elven archers, and, well, fought a beast just now. No offense."

He chuckled. "None taken." Henry paused for a moment, listening to the crunch of their boots as they followed the trail of glowing sparkles left behind when Moss had carried Faiya away from the action. "I missed you, you know. Loads. River's End feels even more colorless without you there."

"I always knew you were a sap." Arya laughed, shaking her head. "I missed you too, Henry. Although admittedly, I didn't think *this* was the way we'd find each other again."

They both laughed at that, continuing their trek through the wintry forests and snow-covered clearings. Eventually, the trail led them to a cave, light spilling from its entrance. Arya felt a presence there, even before she saw anyone, something powerful. She knew if must be the Wynterborn. After all the time they had spent searching for a village, here they were in a cave.

Once they walked inside, they saw that Faiya was propped up against some cushions and fur, and Moss was surrounded by white-haired people dressed in white lace and silk. They each had a hand aimed at the tall Half-Goblin boy.

"Explain yourself, Halfling." A Wynterborn with her long white hair braided over her shoulder demanded, narrowing her icy blue eyes. A crown of ice sat in her hair, so Arya assumed this must be their leader. Beside her stood two large men with ice spears, both of them pointed at Moss.

Arya rushed into the mix, leaving Henry to scoop up Finnigan's limp body. "Don't hurt him!" she shouted.

Half of the group of snow-benders turned, aiming their weapons and hands at her instead.

"And *you* are?" The woman snapped. Her gorgeous icy gown contrasted with her dark skin, making her look celestial, regal. Her icy blue eyes stood out in an almost glowing sort of way.

"I'm Arya from the village of River's End…And this is Henry and our friend Finnigan, a Leprechaun from Clover Town in the Marshwood Clearing." Arya figured her words could buy them some much needed time. "We received word that years ago, a daughter went missing from here. There was a chance that I might be her, but I'm not. We were under the attack of a…" she looked to Henry, who gave her a wide-eyed look, telling her to go on with what she was saying, "beast of some kind."

"But it's gone now." Henry added quickly. "It slinked off into the woods after Arya nearly put it down."

"*You* defeated a Wynterbeast?" Eirwen scoffed. "You're only a girl."

"I'm more than I look." Arya replied, her eyes changing to the icy shade of the eyes of the woman looking at her. A flash of recognition spread across the woman's features and she motioned for her people to lower their readied attacks and weapons.

"Where have you *really* come from, Arya of River's End? Why have you come here?" Her voice was soft, but her eyes were still guarded. Every word held weight.

"I came from River's End," she repeated. "I've been a lot of places since I left there, sure, but that's my home, a Mortal village in the Borderlands."

Eirwen didn't look convinced. "Your Halfling came here with a downed Fae. Did he do that? Scramble her Magyk?"

"No. That was me." Arya hung her head and glanced over Faiya before looking back at the woman made of ice, fire in her eyes. "And he's not *my* Halfling. He's my *friend*."

"Until we receive a message from the Fae saying this girl is authorized to be with you, we'll keep you here. To be safe." She watched Arya, gauging the risk involved as though she was afraid the girl would explode at any moment. "Guards, take them to the holding cell." But before anyone moved, she spoke, "Wait! What of the Leprechaun?"

"He was knocked out by the beast, ma'am." Henry answered, his voice low and filled with shame. "Otherwise, he's unharmed."

Considering it for a moment, the leader of the Wynterborn called her guards once again. One wave of her wrist and all of them except Faiya and Finn were in icy bonds that wouldn't melt and tossed into a snowy cage.

Arya landed in a pile of fluff, groaning at the sudden cold as her hair flushed white again. Henry's teeth chattered and Moss couldn't feel his toes. After a few moments sitting in the white flakes, though, Arya was immune. Her Magyk tapped into that of the Wynterborn and shielded her from the effects of the cold.

Henry found himself sitting there and staring at his childhood friend. After all of his years in River's End, growing up alongside her, seeing her this way was strange. She was different now, more powerful. This was the Magyk she'd been cut off from, these abilities. This was what the Mortals had stolen from her. In their greed, they'd taken everything from Arya and in turn, forced her to be something she never could: normal.

Though they were barely even touching, Henry's new beastly warmth enveloped her. He'd always been warmer than her, but his condition made him even more so, a heater in their small and chilly cell. Henry reached out, using the foot of icy chain between his bound wrists to take Arya's hand in his own. His fingers were long and warm, his hands rough from years of working with his father as a blacksmith.

Henry intertwined his fingers with Arya's smaller, colder ones and gave her hand a reassuring squeeze. His golden eyes glimmered and when she looked up at him, even where they were, in an icy prison held by the Wynterborn until they could figure out this whole disaster, she still brought a smile to his handsome features.

"I missed you," he spoke softly. He could say it a million times and he still wouldn't have said it enough.

"I missed you, too." She had, every day. The necklace around her neck seemed to pulse with warmth as she said it, a silent reminder that it was still there, even after everything she'd been through.

"So, how's Recensere? Aside from the Spyders and Elves and beasts, I mean?"

"You're here, aren't you?" Arya giggled.

Henry shrugged, his thumb wandering across her smooth skin. "Haven't seen much of it yet."

Arya furrowed her brows. He had gone all the way there, hadn't he? Did he not remember anything?

Henry reached up to rub the back of his neck, but was stopped by the chain linking his wrists together. He exhaled a long breath, preparing to give an explanation. "I don't remember any of it. Aside from waking up to you, with your eyes locked on mine and your Magyk fixing the mistakes I made."

"You didn't make any mistakes," Arya whispered. Her eyes shifted from their joined hands to his eyes, now golden with the dangerous Magyk he was harboring inside him.

"I wouldn't say that..." Henry forced his eyes away from hers. "I....should have trusted you, that you would be alright without me. You're doing fine. You *would* be doing fine if I hadn't shown up and —"

"Don't." Arya stopped him with a single look. "Don't say that. I'm glad you're here, despite it all. I'm glad you came, even if maybe it wasn't under the greatest circumstances. I...need you, Henry."

"You don't *need* me."

"I do." She rested her head against his shoulder and he rested his atop her head. "You know I do."

"Not as much as *I* need *you*." He fixed his gaze on her boot-covered feet and the fine brown leather armor she was wearing. There was a story in every asset of her outfit. The fur wrapped around her shoulders, the necklace around her neck, the golden band with Elvish Runes fastened around her wrist. She had been through things Henry could never understand.

"Tell me about what happened," Arya asked after a long silence between them.

"Believe me, you don't want to know."

"Tell me."

"Arya—"

"Don't 'Arya' me, Henry Smith. Tell me what happened. You don't have to hold it in. Maybe I could help make it better if you tell me how."

He hesitated, quiet for a long time, but eventually, he decided she was right. "I had a vision, alright? A stupid vision like the Sacreds or whatever they call themselves."

Henry was frustrated, but not with her, with himself, with the situation he was in. He was angry with the Mortals in River's End for messing things up in the first place, for making him think he could have this perfect Mortal girl that was never really Mortal in the first place.

But he didn't say any of that.

"Okay, so you had a vision. Of what?" Arya, ever the patient one of the pair, was gentle with him. She could tell he was beating himself up inside, and she was the only one in their village who understood how to handle him when he got like this.

"Of you, Arya. Of you running through the woods for your life." He sighed. "I packed up my things, grabbed my father's sword, and hiked through the Borderlands to meet with a Frynge Wytch. She showed me a vision of you trying to escape from a growling beast of some sort...which I now realize was *me*." He shook his head. "I...I don't remember much beyond that, but what I *do* remember wasn't so pleasant..."

"And then she cursed you." Arya spoke softly. She picked her head off of his shoulder and tugged aside the collar of his armor, revealing a burn that resembled the Moons of Recensere.

Henry squirmed under her gentle fingers. Even the most tentative touch hurt like a hot branding iron, not unlike one of his many smithing burns from over the years. Henry trudged deeper into his clouded memory and forced himself to remember what had happened the moment after he promised to do anything for the girl sitting beside him.

He remembered his transformation hurting more than anything he'd ever felt or ever would feel. Magyk filled his veins, breaking every piece of his body before putting it back together again.

His vision and memory went hazy after that, fogged over with the effects of whatever the Wytch had done to him, but he had a sinking feeling in the pit of his stomach that he had killed her. And he didn't know how many others along the way to where he was now.

"I think I killed her, Arya…" He whispered. "Probably others on the way here. I don't remember."

"It's not your fault, whatever happened. She tricked you. None of what happened until you found me was anything you could control. And I promise, whatever she did to you, we'll find a way to fix it."

Moss, who had been silent as they talked, didn't really know what to say about any of it. Wytches were tricky; he knew that. In fact, they were part of the reason the kingdom was in shambles. He also was too cold to think straight at the moment, though, so he was really hoping they would get some news from the Faerfolk Glade soon one way or the other.

Maybe if they were lucky, Faedella would vouch for them.

After catching up with Henry, Arya fell asleep on his shoulder, but he forced himself to stay awake. He was afraid of letting himself slip into that dark and dangerous place again. He didn't want to hurt Arya or anyone else, so until he was sure he wasn't going to turn back into a Wynterbeast, he was determined to keep his eyes open, no matter how badly he wanted to drift off.

"She's not telling me something." Henry spoke softly, careful not to wake the sleeping girl on his shoulder. Her eyes were closed, drowsy breaths flowing in and out of her evenly. Henry had spent enough quiet nights with her to know she was a heavy sleeper. "Care to enlighten me?"

"It's not really my tale to tell." Moss fiddled with his fingers, studying the Mortal boy's beastly features. Henry's teeth were just a little too sharp and his eyes were just a little too golden. No one had told Moss what had happened to the beast, but looking at Henry...he had a decent idea.

"Listen, she's not going to tell me if something is wrong. But...I need to know, okay? And it'll come out sooner or later, so I recommend you tell me now before it becomes an imminent problem."

"I don't know much; I haven't been traveling with them for very long..." The Half-Goblin sighed. "But what I *do* know is that it's not good."

"What do you mean by that?" A thick lump formed in Henry's throat. Maybe there had been a mistake. A misdiagnosis. Even looking at her while she slept, it didn't feel like anything was monumentally wrong.

"From what I've heard, she has about a Moons' Cycle to figure out...where she's supposed to be. I don't know. Probably less than that now that they've been traveling. I wish I could tell you more, but, like I said, I haven't been with them for all that long. It's a good thing you got here when you did. We need all the help we can get."

"Isn't there anything else we can do? A Witch or a Spellcaster or *someone* must have something..."

"All I know is that I'm going with them to Blackrock and that they're supposed to be meeting up with one of the Centaurs there, but until then...the longer we stay here..." Moss let his eyes linger on the sleeping girl. He'd only known her for a few days, but she had a way of leaving an impression on people.

Losing her wouldn't be easy for anyone, but especially not for Henry.

"We better get out of here soon." Henry eyed up the lock to their cage and then examined the cuffs around his wrists.

Maybe, just maybe, there was a way to get out of them just in case the Fae gave the Wynterborn the wrong answer…

TANGLED DEEPER

Reading the book had taken quite a toll on Selena Moon. Her sleep schedule had been blown to hell. She couldn't concentrate, couldn't listen to music, couldn't look at bright lights or stand too close to the freezer. Little things would send her into a sensory overload, a frenzy of sorts. She would shut down and lock herself in her dark bedroom, lying beneath the covers until the world stopped spinning and shouting at her.

Delphinus and Johnny, rightfully, felt like they were walking on eggshells every time they were around her. The trio had been spending more and more time together in hopes of finding something in the book that had to do with the Eclypse, but no matter how hard Selena tried to search for that specific information, she was always drawn back into the story of Arya and Finnigan and Henry, forced to read the words of the powerful being that had created the book.

Selena tried to lock it away, to hide it from her sight, but the longer she avoided reading it, the more time she spent staring at the Runes as they rearranged themselves on the page, changing into something she, but not the boys, could read.

"Selena? Babe?" Johnny was gentle with her, trying to rouse her from her thoughts. She had been staring at the wall of his living room for quite some time. "Are you okay?"

She blinked a few times, eyelids slowly closing over her silver eyes. Once she had seemed to register the question, she nodded.

"Do you need something?" Delphinus prodded just as tentatively as his human friend had. These past few weeks had been more productive for him than they had been for Selena. He had found a way to decipher the Hevynspeak Prophecies. Just because he couldn't remember how to speak the language anymore didn't mean he couldn't translate them into something he *could* remember. That language happened to be Latin, which he then translated to English so they could use them to learn about the Eclypse and how to prevent it from tearing his friends and their world apart.

"Pepsi." Selena replied quicker this time. She was starting to snap out of the deep haze that the book put her under. "Please."

"No problem." He nodded and walked over to Johnny's kitchen to grab a cold one from the fridge.

Selena curled into Johnny's warmth, her legs settling on top of his, and her head finding a comfortable spot in the crook of his neck. He wrapped an arm around her waist and pulled her closer to him, pressing a long kiss to her forehead while Delphinus retrieved three cans of Pepsi, one for each member of the trio.

"You said Henry has a Mark like mine."

"Different curse." Delphinus piped up, ever the knowledgeable one on the Recenserean Curses. "Similar Mark, but different effects."

Johnny shot Delphinus a look that told the know-it-all to shut up and let him talk. "Maybe you and I are like Arya and Henry. Maybe the cure to his curse could help break mine and then when the Eclypse comes, we won't have anything to worry about."

"Yeah, except Arya isn't a Starchild and Henry isn't a Marked One."

"I get it. They're different. But you can't help but notice the parallels."

Delphinus shrugged and opened his can of Pepsi, taking a few tentative sips. He didn't care for the taste, but the sugar helped his human body stay awake. Having his powers back in addition to his white hair would be extremely helpful to this process, but that wasn't plausible at the moment, thus, he had to make do with what they had.

"I don't know." Selena mumbled into Johnny's neck. "I need..."

"What do you need, babe? Tell me what you need."

"Can I sleep...in...?"

"My room?" Johnny asked.

Selena nodded, clinging to her boyfriend like a koala. He adjusted his hold on her and carried her down the stairs to his room in the basement. She liked how cozy it was, how it smelled like him. It made her feel safe even with everything going on inside of and around her.

Once Johnny had her tucked away, he walked back upstairs to where Delphinus was sitting, Pepsi in hand, a blank look on his angelic features. Like it or not, the guy was sort of his girlfriend's guardian angel in a way. Except, where he came from, what humans know as 'Angels' are actually a divine creature called a 'Hallowyng.'

Delphinus' true home was a place called the Hevynrealm, a vantage point from where the Hallowyngs could look down on Terra or Incanto or any other realm they chose. Delphinus remembered those things, the basics, his home, it was his memories that were still much too scrambled to make sense of. Everything after departing from the Hevynrealm was a blur until he met Johnny and Selena.

Johnny didn't pay too much mind to all of the complicated stuff, though. All he cared about was Selena, and at the moment, she wasn't doing so well, so it was up to the other two to figure out how to fix her, or at the very least, how to prevent her condition from getting worse.

Johnny had a very bad feeling it would have something to do with destroying the large leather-bound book sitting on the table.

Chapter 16

NEGOTIATION IN WATERY DEPTHS

When the next morning came, so did a Raven from the Faer-folk Glade with a note from Faedella. The scroll was tied with a golden ribbon, and when the leader of the Wynterborn unrolled it, the tension left her stiff shoulders.

"To Eirwen of the Wynterborn,

My daughter, Faiya, has been missing from the Glade for a few days now. I suspect she went against my wishes and followed two of the members of the group you described, Finnigan and Arya. I did not know she had left, but she's there now. In all honesty, I believe Arya and Finnigan and whoever else has joined them need all the help they can get; The girl's life depends on it.

As for the problem you described that's affecting my daughter, tell the Leprechaun that this is Fae Fever. He'll know how to fix it and get the foreign Magyk out of her system.

Tell Arya I wish her the best.

-Faedella of the Fae"

Eirwen walked to the cell she was keeping her shivering prisoners in. Arya, the girl who now had white hair that matched the Wynterborn, stirred in the sunlight shining through the crystalline bars that held them captive. With a flick of the woman's wrist, the bonds binding their hands exploded, shattering instantly. At the sound, Henry jolted awake, his muscled arms wrapping protectively around Arya, ready to attack whatever was threatening them.

However, when he looked around to see his drowsy friends were unharmed and the binds that were holding him were gone,

161

he calmed. Arya felt his body lose its tension. She rubbed his arm a few times, gently reassuring him.

"Leprechaun," Eirwen called confidently.

Finnigan jolted to attention. "Yes, yer majesty?" He'd woken up some time before with a massive headache due to the events of the previous night, but otherwise he seemed unharmed.

"Your friend has Fae Fever. Faedella said you could fix her."

It took a second for the words to process, the world still spinning a bit, but eventually, he replied, "That I can, with the supplies in our packs. Hope ye didn't throw them out in the snow, yer majesty."

"They're outside your cage, wee one." The Queen looked down on him as he struggled to stand.

Finnigan was even shorter this morning than he had been the previous morning. Arya noticed it, too. When she stood up beside him, she could almost see over the top of his red hair.

Kneeling beside one of the large supply bundles, Finnigan shuffled through the gear he had packed. Kisa was a smart Centaur; she knew at some point the pair would need healing Magyk, and because of the Centaurs' close proximity to the Fae, they had an abundance of vials and things from their neighbors.

Henry stood back with Arya and Moss while Finnigan hovered over Faiya, a vial of golden liquid in his hand. It was glowing and sparkling, the liquid stirring itself around in its corked glass vessel.

Finnigan used careful fingers, and what little of his own Magyk he could gather, to lift the healing essence out of the bottle, into the air, and then lower it onto Faiya. Once it had mingled with her face for a few seconds, he pulled it into the air once more. With it, came a cloud of silver, which rumbled with thunder, fizzles of power flashing white like lightning.

While Faiya finally stirred from her sleep, all of the Wynterborn looked up at the cloud in horror, backing away from the menacing Magyk that had been expelled from the Fae. Then, once it dissipated into the air, the Wynterborn all looked to Arya pointedly.

"You brought this Magyk here," accused a white-haired man.

"What *are* you, Arya of the Borderlands?" Eirwen asked, eyes narrowed. "What are you, really?"

"I...I don't know!" The girl replied. "I'm sorry...I didn't mean to!"

Henry could feel his anger boiling just below the surface, his need to protect her growing the longer they looked at her. He took a step forward, a low growl rumbling in his chest.

Arya's cold hand gave his larger, warmer one a squeeze, calming him down a bit, but not entirely. These emotions weren't his own. Yes, he was restless and adventurous, but he had never been quick-tempered. That Wytch had changed Arya's best friend in ways she would never forgive her for.

Eirwen looked over the girl for a few more seconds. Obviously, she couldn't stay there any longer; She could be a danger to the Wynterborn.

"Arya of the Borderlands, take your things and your people and leave this place. We cannot help you."

"Okay," Arya replied quietly, nodding. She and the others hurried to gather their things, making sure everything was accounted for before they left the mouth of the cave.

Faiya, who was still just waking up, was less than enthused about moving this early, but Moss had volunteered to carry her as far as she needed, for which she thanked him, but politely declined his offer. It took her a few minutes to find her footing, but eventually she did, settling into a steady rhythm beside the rest of her traveling companions.

Finnigan discovered, as the group walked through the wintry woodlands, that he was having a bit of trouble keeping up with them. His legs were shorter, he realized. *He* was shorter. About three or four inches shorter than Arya, who was, or had previously been, the shortest member of the party. To make up for it, however, he had a bit more of that Leprechaun pep in his step.

By the time the sun was in the center of the sky, the woods stopped being wintry. Their boots began to sink into the soft dirt and then mud of the paths as the air grew more humid. Moss took a breath of fresh air, relieved to be near his homeland once again.

"You know," the Half-Goblin surveyed his surroundings, "if I remember correctly, there's a bit of a shortcut not far from here. If we took it, I bet we'd be in Blackrock before nightfall."

"All in favor?" Henry asked. There weren't any objections from the others, as none of them were particularly keen on the idea of sleeping on the ground for the third night in a row.

So, on they walked until they came across a path in the dirt. Soon, though, the dirt turned into sand and they could hear the ocean once more. Gulls called and waves lapped against the shore. Arya felt another change brewing within her the closer they got to it.

What Moss had forgotten in his excitement to get home after a few years of being away was that the coast in these parts was not uninhabited. In fact, there was a variety of creatures that lived there. Creatures that did *not* take kindly to strangers.

As they approached the beach, the group, felt a lull. The call was weak enough that most of them were able to fight it off. Henry's new beastly blood resisted the urge to walk closer. Moss had heard the calls before, and his Goblin ears were unaffected. Arya's fluctuating Magyk protected her from the mythical force, and Faiya was much too powerful to be stirred from the path, despite the fact that she was still recovering.

Finnigan, however, took off at a run.

He ran for the waters like his life depended on it, kicking off his boots, tearing off his fur, and ripping off the jackets he was wearing. In his shirt, suspenders, and trousers, he ran as fast as he could until he was standing at the edge of the waves.

"Finnigan wait!"

"Where are you going?!"

"Oh no…" Moss murmured, suddenly remembering why he didn't often take this shortcut.

Arya and the others followed, sprinting after him, but their speed did not compare to the Leprechaun's. He was too fast for them; his Leprechaun speed had decided to return to him at the worst possible time.

Finnigan's feet were planted in the gentle waters at the edge of the beach. He stared out at the waves with lust in his eyes, shining and unfaltering. Arya tried to snap him out of it, calling out to him very loudly, but it didn't do anything. He wouldn't budge from the shore, and he was too far from them, as they knew, for any of them to stop him from walking further into the sea.

These were the Syrens, Faiya realized, her eyes widening, the tricky creatures that had a habit of leading Mortal men with greed in their hearts to their deaths. Around these parts, there had been a shortage of Mortal men and the Syrens had turned their tempting to another kind, or really, *any* other kind that dared to wander near their lands.

So Finnigan waded into the depths, pushing, struggling against the water. Just as Arya and Henry cleared the edge of the trees, Finnigan's red curls went under. Arya screamed, running even faster, but Henry latched onto her arm.

"Arya, there's nothing we can do." Henry tried to pull her back, his golden eyes glowing protectively. He had to stop her from doing the thing he could tell she was about to do. They had switched roles. Now, Henry was the one that wanted to play it safe and Arya was the one tugging to break free of protection.

She had to do this for Finnigan. He would have done it for her.

"He's right, Arya. They're Syrens. If you go after him, you'll die too." Faiya warned as she and Moss emerged from the trees after the first pair.

Arya looked to Henry and then to Faiya and then to Moss, her eyes growing bluer and bluer by the second. "I have to try." So, Arya broke free of Henry's hold and ripped off all of the heavy furs that would only drag her down.

She ran down the beach, kicking off her shoes as she evaded Henry's desperate hands reaching to grab onto her, and dove into the water.

She plunged into the raging depths, and as she pushed her head under the surface, she felt a searing sensation on the sides of her neck. It burned like a hot iron, fresh and sharp against her soft flesh. When the pain faded, it was replaced by a gentle tingling sensation instead. Arya pushed through the waters, desperate to go deeper, to find Finnigan's fiery head of hair in the clear blue depths.

A variety of fish swam by her as she dove down, down, down. She wasn't sure how much time had passed since she had gone under, but she noticed that her lungs weren't screaming for air, like she'd expected them to. Instead, the oxygen flowed in and out of her freely, through the new openings in her neck.

Gills, she realized. She had *gills*. The tips of her hair caught in the corner of her eye, redder than they had ever been. It wasn't Leprechaun red, like it had been while she'd slept beside Finnigan. Instead, her naturally brown tresses had taken on a color that rivaled that of roses and cherries and all the red things she had been deprived of in her life in River's End. This was the red of the Syrens.

Her feet developed a thin webbing between her toes that pushed her on faster. Her fingers had them too. It was an odd sensation, but it propelled her through the water like a frog, faster than she could have dived as a Mortal girl or any other creature whose Magyk she'd borrowed before.

Finally, she found him. Finnigan was drifting there in the depths, lifeless. Bubbles clung to his face in little clumps, his now-oversized clothes were soaked, drifting around his lanky form, and his hair was as red as it was in the sunlight, curls reaching and retracting as he bobbed. Around him, there were Syrens, their arms and legs covered in glimmering seafoam green scales, their fingers and toes webbed like Arya's were. All of their other suspended prisoners held down by strings of seaweed, tying the victims down like anchors tethered to their ankles.

Arya approached them cautiously, listening as their voices echoed in her head.

"*You don't belong here, girl. Leave this place.*" One of them hissed. Arya couldn't hear the voice out loud. All she could *physically* hear were the sounds of the ocean, but in her mind, the words resounded, loud and real.

"*You took my friend. I'm not leaving without him.*" Arya told them, her seafoam green eyes narrowing at the creatures around her.

"*Then you will die,*" hissed another. A male Syren rushed at her with a trident, its sharp blades pointed at Arya's neck.

She screamed, and through the water rippled waves of sound that caused all of the Syrens to shriek in distress. Arya noticed their discomfort and rushed forward, ready to launch a screaming attack at whoever challenged her next.

"*A Banshee in these parts?*" asked one, confused. An army of green eyes narrowed at the foreign creature and they swam closer, examining her.

At that moment, the Merfolk emerged from the depths of the sea to find out what all of the commotion was about, their powerful tails propelling them towards the source of the trouble. Arya looked around, comparing the variations of creatures surrounding her.

The Syrens had hair the color of cherries and eyes as seafoam green as her own, their bottom halves split into two limbs, whereas the Merfolk, who looked much friendlier than their Wycked counterparts, had teal hair that faded into a deep royal blue at the ends and tails in the place of legs, their sparkling scales catching the light in the prettiest ways.

One of the Syrens swam up to Arya, quickly closing the distance between them. The creature's long webbed fingers cupped the girl's face as she studied the stranger carefully. Arya felt her feet beginning to bind together, but it was not with a seaweed chain as she had feared. No, they were adhering to themselves, a layer of scales growing over her bare Mortal legs and forcing them into one joint limb with a fin at the end.

"She has the scream of a Banshee, the hair of a Syren, and the tail of a Mer." Stated one of the Mermen. He was a large and muscled man with broad shoulders and a thick blue beard. His hair was long, teal and blue, and the curls drifted down past his shoulders. He had so many tattoos that under any other circumstances, she would have mistaken him for a Mortal sailor. His blue eyes pierced her, seeming to peer directly into her soul.

Her heart pounded.

"The Banshees went extinct long ago." The Syren that was holding her face continued to look over Arya uncertainly. *"And now she comes here demanding the release of our prey."*

"Let the girl go, Nix," the Merman demanded. *"She's done you no wrong. Your kind stole her friend. Release him and let it be."*

"Speak for your own kind, Kainalu. You are not king of the sea, despite what you may believe." Nix hissed.

Arya felt like a child standing between her bickering parents, as had happened several times in her childhood in River's End. John and Katherine loved each other, sure, but they had their fair share of arguments. Now that Arya knew that they had kept secrets not only from her, but also from each other, she knew why they were so prone to bickering.

*"Don't put this on **me**, Nix. You've been kidnapping innocents for your collection long before my mother left me her throne. This girl is getting her friend back, and if you don't cooperate, I'll free **all** of your prisoners."*

*"You wouldn't **dare**,"* she hissed back at him.

He raised his trident and puffed out his chest, confidence consuming his muscled figure. There were many Merfolk there, and just as many Syrens. Arya didn't want to be the cause of an underwater war, but to get Finnigan back to safety, perhaps that was what she had to do. Though it was obvious as she observed them that their problems were deep-rooted and hadn't originated from the changing girl with the Banshee's voice that came into their lagoon.

"Merfolk, free the Syren prisoners," Kainalu ordered. On his command, the Merfolk sliced all of the bonds holding the bodies suspended underwater. They began to float to the surface. *"Girl, take your friend. Go now, before things get worse."*

Arya nodded, not one to argue, and swam to Finnigan. Her new tail was even faster than her webbed toes had been. She reached his body with ease, but found he wasn't breathing. None of the prisoners were, and yet, their hearts were beating. Panicked, Arya pressed her lips to Finnigan's. She forced a breath into his unmoving lungs and his eyes tore open. He gasped for air, but realized once his lips left Arya's that there wasn't any air to gasp for.

Arya pressed her lips to his again, giving him another spurt of air that would hopefully get him to the surface. He wasn't entirely sure what had happened or where he was. He just remembered the beach and then...

Syrens had done this, and he had been too weak to resist their call to the sea, bidding him to come closer. He'd been tempted by visions. Now, he couldn't quite remember what they had been of, but he had a sinking feeling it had something to do with the very activity he was doing currently: kissing Arya.

Had it not been for her, he surely would have died. Or at the very least, he would have ended up a trophy for all eternity. That was what the Syrens did. They kept their prisoners until they needed them for their dark Magyk. Or, he shuddered at the thought, for food. And now, all of the former prisoners, who had been frozen by their time in the sea, were floating freely to the surface.

Arya helped Finnigan out of the water, but quickly found that she was stuck, given her new tail. Henry rushed into the water to meet her, already soaking wet from his attempts in vain to rescue her, tears glimmering in his golden eyes. There had been no reason for him to learn how to swim in River's End; the water at their turn of the river was barely deep enough to reach his hips, and therefore, when Arya dove after Finnigan, he'd been all but helpless to stop her, afraid of drowning, but even *more* afraid of losing her again.

She gasped as her gills painfully resealed into her neck. It burned even worse than when they had formed, and when the pain was gone, she curled against Henry's chest, breathing heavily as she readjusted to using her nose and mouth again. He slowly lifted her out of the water, stumbling due to the weight of her tail. Without his new beastly strength, he doubted he'd have been able to carry her at all.

The freed prisoners hugged each other as they reunited with family and friends, stumbling on their way out of the depths that had held them prisoner for years, if not decades.

Arya feared, as she looked out on the waters, that Kainalu would be killed in the battle raging silently under the sea. She didn't doubt that he was strong, but she knew the Syrens were angry enough to put up a fight. Her fears subsided, however, when, in a large fountain of salty waters bursting forth from the sea, Kainalu was carried in the waves, unharmed and upright, almost standing in the depths.

"You have no reason to fear, citizens of Recensere. The fight of a thousand Merfolk did free you from the Syrens' mighty grip. And this girl was the catalyst." Kainalu spoke with his mouth rather than his thoughts this time, and his voice sounded the same as it had in her head.

"I didn't do anything." Arya tried to tell him, her sea form still affecting her ability to walk.

Though Henry's arms were beginning to strain, he didn't falter or let her slip. He'd carry her all the way to Blackrock, if she needed him to.

"Child, I've been waiting for an excuse to fight the Syrens for years." Kainalu laughed a hearty laugh and raised his trident. "They will not be making trouble for quite some time, I think."

"Well, in that case, you're welcome." Arya's legs finally emerged from the powerful tail that had replaced them as it split right up the middle, her feet reforming from the fins that were attached to it. Kainalu wrinkled his brows in confusion at the sight of the girl changing before his eyes.

"What *are* you?" This marked about the hundredth time, it felt like, that Arya had been asked that question.

"I don't know," she replied once again, still not sure what answer to give him or anyone else that wondered about her. "I'm still hoping to find that out."

"I, too, am one who changes: a Halfling." Kainalu admitted. He walked onto the shore, his tail becoming legs much easier than Arya's had. Henry set Arya on her feet as the last of the red faded from her hair. Her eyes, however, remained blue. "My mother used her sea Magyk to complete my transformation so I could assume her throne. And now, I'm on my way to visit the High King Valens, to seek his aid in ridding the Syrens from the Recenserean seas. Their Wycked ways have more than banished them in my book."

"Thank ye, yer majesty." Finnigan bowed to the tall man standing before him.

"Don't mention it." The Merman smiled and gave the Leprechaun a friendly pat on the back. "Maybe our paths will cross again. I hope you find your place."

And with that, he left them, walking down the paths to the Square to seek out the word of the High King.

The herd of clueless Mortals and other assorted Magykfolk that were standing in the sand listened to Moss' directions to get out to the Borderlands so they could build a new life for themselves now that they were free from the Syrens' grip after nearly two decades. And then they were gone too, leaving only Arya, Moss, Henry, Faiya, and Finnigan, standing in a daze on the beach.

Before they headed out again, the group stopped to dry their wet boots and change into clothes that weren't soaked. Henry helped Arya wipe down her armor and then reassemble it, tying all the strings and fastening all the straps. And then, once they had everything together, they continued to walk away from the beach. Blackrock wasn't far from there. The run-in with the Syrens had set them behind a few hours, and though they thought they'd make it to the mines before dusk fell, it became evident a little while later that they weren't going to be able to get there after all. So, once the sun was halfway set, they picked a secluded spot to settle down for the night.

The group set up camp in a thicket of trees. The mines were close enough that the clinging and clanging of the Glowyr could be heard, and though they were indeed near their destination, they knew all too well how dangerous it was to travel at night, even such a short distance.

Moss helped Henry start a fire while Finnigan unpacked some bread rolls as well as some preserved meat from their supplies. While the boys cooked over the fire, Faiya sat on a fallen log next to Arya.

"They care about you, you know." Faiya watched as Henry helped Finnigan grill for the group and Moss gathered more dry wood, tending carefully to the flames.

"I'm lucky like that, I guess." Arya's eyes lingered on Finnigan before her gaze found Henry again.

Faiya was quiet for a long moment before speaking quietly. "*I* care about you…" Faiya looked to Arya and brushed a piece of golden-tipped hair out of her face. Arya's proximity to the Fae was causing her to take on some of Faiya's traits, but neither of them minded all that much. In fact, sitting in the firelight beside her, Faiya could have sworn Arya was glowing.

"I know you do." Arya smiled softly and rested her hand atop the Fae's. "Thank you for coming all this way. I'd already be dead if it wasn't for you."

Faiya wasn't sure what to say to that, so she opted not to say anything at all, instead staring at the flickering flames, watching as they danced under the star-filled sky. "There aren't any men where I'm from," she noted quietly, earning a thoughtful hum from Arya. "All of the Fae in my village are women."

"I suppose I should have noticed that."

"Male Fae don't exist. Well, some do, but they don't start out that way. I didn't expect you to know that, all things considered." She was quiet for a moment before continuing. "When you left with Finnigan, it felt like a piece of my soul went off with you. I knew I had to do something to help. I'm sorry if it caused any trouble."

"This whole trip has been nothing but trouble, but that's not your fault. If anything, it's mine for crossing the Veil in the first place."

"What, and miss out on any chance of returning to where you belong? No, you're meant to be here somewhere. There's someone waiting out there for you, someone who will love you." What Faiya didn't say was that she knew for a fact there were already people in the Magyklands, people at their very camp, even, that already did.

Arya couldn't help but let her eyes linger on Henry when she finally replied. "Yeah. Yeah, I think you're right."

●◐○○○◐●●

Once they'd eaten, Arya set up her sleeping roll, and Henry, who didn't have one, hesitantly squirmed inside it. She crawled in next to him.

"Arya..." He murmured as she found a comfortable spot. His quiet voice was almost swallowed up by the constant chirping of the crickets in the trees surrounding them. "Maybe this isn't the best idea..."

"Why?"

"Well, I just...I'm not sure about my curse. I'm... I'm afraid I'll hurt you."

"You won't. I promise you won't. I can handle myself, you know."

"It's not that—" Henry interjected, but Arya shushed him by pressing a finger against his lips.

"I trust you. Do you trust me?" she whispered.

Henry was quiet for a moment, nodding. He kissed Arya's forehead and adjusted so his arms wound further around her waist. "Of course I trust you…I'm just not sure I trust myself anymore…"

Arya sank deeper into Henry's warmth. Though the circumstances that brought him to her weren't exactly ideal, she was glad he was there with her.

At least now, she would be able to properly say goodbye to him when the time came.

Chapter 17

THE GOBLINS' HOME

Arya awoke to the snores of Henry and Moss, the former rumbling just above her ear, and the other coming from the sleeping Half-Goblin, who was still slumbering a few sleeping rolls away.

"Good morning, princess," Finnigan whispered, making eye contact with her from his bundle, a few feet from her own.

"Good morning, Finn," she whispered back, smiling softly. He reached one of his little Leprechaun hands out for hers and she met him in the middle. For the first time, Arya noticed just how small his hands had become.

"How'd ye sleep?"

"Fine, you?"

Henry let out a loud snore, an arm tightening around Arya. Finnigan chuckled to himself, tilting his head toward the sleeping boy. "I've slept better."

"Sorry." Arya smiled sheepishly, but Finnigan only laughed.

When she awoke in the next roll over, Faiya was quiet for a long time, listening to the sounds of the woods: the birds calling, the twigs snapping, and very faintly in the distance, the constant pinging and ringing of the blacksmith workshops and mines not far from their makeshift camp.

It wasn't much longer until they'd be there, in Moss' home, finally returning him to where he belonged after his years of servitude to the High Elves, who, Moss had informed them, were just as racist and awful as they'd heard.

Once all of their things were gathered, and their fire stomped out, they began their hike through the trees, following the clashing of metal to where the Goblins and Glowyr dwelled.

While the Glowyr dug and dug and dug all day, searching for treasures and other valuable resources, the Goblins crafted fine goods from their bounties, trading with travelers that came seeking Silver, Gold, Bronze, and priceless jewels. These were also the mines that provided the rest of the kingdom with steel for their weapons.

It was a very busy place with a system in motion, and standing in the center of the buzzing hive was a Centaur. Agathon looked the same as he had when last they'd seen him. His shoulder-length hair was arranged in braids, a few wooden and silver beads mixed in for decoration.

"Perfect timing." He approached the group with slow but confident strides. "I arrived last night."

"We would have, but we ran into some of the Syrens and Merfolk and may have inadvertently started a war under the waves." Arya told the Centaurs' second-in-command.

"No one likes the Syrens." Agathon chuckled. "I wouldn't worry too much. You've done the oceans a favor."

"And ye saved me life, so there's that." Finnigan gave Arya a playful little nudge. It was then that she noticed he was standing at her shoulder. She had to look down a whole head to talk to him.

"You're so—"

"Short. I know." Finnigan looked up at her, crossing his arms. "Don't remind me."

"I thought you *wanted* to be short again." Arya chuckled, watching as his freckled cheeks flushed pinker. "You've been complaining about it this whole time."

"Well…" Finnigan was saved by Agathon, who was an impatient Centaur.

"Arya, do you feel any different, being here?"

The girl shook her head. "I'm sure I have a place somewhere, but this isn't it."

"Shame. It would have been nice to be neighbors." Moss hung his head. He realized what being here meant. It meant his leg of the journey was over, and though he was beyond relieved to be home after so long, he couldn't help but be the tiniest bit sad that he'd have to say goodbye to them. He became sadder when he realized that in Arya's case, this could be her final farewell. "Stay for lunch. My Mother will want to meet all of you."

"Thank you." Arya smiled softly at the tall Halfling.

He nodded and then led them into one of the houses tucked into the hills surrounding the mines. She could tell by the shapes of the rocky homes that these places had been dug out of the mountain by the miners, but now that the ore was gone, they were useless as resource deposits and instead made good homes, once they had been furnished.

The door of Moss' home was made of fine wood the Goblins had gotten from a trade with the Lumberjacks of the North, a group of big, burly creatures who earned their keep in Recensere by trading the wood of their ever-growing trees for goods and services from all over the kingdom. The doorknob was gilded in glittering gemstones. Even the window appeared to be crystalline instead of glass.

Inside the home, a fire was burning in the finished fireplace, the flames warm and orange and casting a cozy light over the room. There was a Goblin woman, much shorter and skinnier than Moss, sitting in the chair in front of the fire. She had knitting needles in her hands, bony fingers manipulating the yarn into what looked a large blanket. At the sound of the door creaking, she looked up, peering over the rims of her glasses at the strangers that had entered her home unannounced.

"Moss?" she gasped and tears took form in her eyes. Her face changed quickly from confusion to joy. She cast the knitting project aside and rushed into his arms. Crying, she stroked a frail hand through her son's thick green hair.

"Hey, Mom." His voice was soft, content. After everything they had escaped, endured, he finally sounded at peace. He finally *felt* at peace. "I'm sorry it took me so long to find my way back."

"Don't you dare apologize. I'm so sorry," she sobbed, gripping him tightly. "I'm sorry I believed the High Elves' lies. I'm sorry I let you go to that...*place*. If I hadn't—"

"It's not your fault. They're awfully good at scaring people into doing what they want." Moss was, unfortunately, speaking from experience. "I'm here now, though, and that's all that matters. The Wood Elves are working to fix what the High Elves have done."

Ruby, Moss' mother, wasn't sure how to put her emotions into words, so she stayed quiet, finally releasing Moss after holding him fiercely for several long moments. She sniffled and wiped at her tears before turning to face the other guests that had entered her home. "I suspect he didn't manage to get here alone. Care to introduce yourselves?"

"I'm Arya." Arya offered her hand but instead found herself in the Goblin's arms, being hugged very tightly. The same went for Finnigan.

"Me name's Finnigan, Ma'am. From Clover Town."

"I'm Henry Smith." He paused for a moment before adding, "From River's End."

"Faiya of the Faerfolk Glade, at your service." Faiya curtsied politely.

Agathon ducked through the doorway, his tall Centaur body barely fitting into the narrow dwelling. "Agathon of the Centaurs, Milady." He bowed, an arm crossed over his bare chest.

Ruby smiled at all of these strangers in her house, the people who had brought her son back to her. She was quiet for a few

179

moments, studying each of their faces before suddenly remembering the pot on her stove. "SOUP! Let's get you all some soup!"

Arya jolted at Ruby's sudden shout, but Moss only smiled softly. Even after all of the time since he'd seen her last, his mother hadn't changed a bit. He helped set the table, getting a spoon for each of them while his mother ladled bowls of soup for each of her unexpected guests.

Over fresh vegetable stew and bread, the company discussed their adventure with Ruby, who was both concerned about the things that had happened thus far and also amazed that this unlikely group had managed to come all that way on their own. She was also worried about Arya, but the girl tried to put on a smile for Moss' mother despite the dull pain slowly blossoming in her head.

While they sat there, Henry had his hand clasped tightly around Arya's, his thumb rubbing steady circles on the back of her hand. He had never been this touchy back before they'd left River's End, but she wasn't opposed to the affection.

"So, you come from Arya's village?" Ruby asked, looking at the Mortal. "River's End, did you say?"

"Yes, ma'am." Henry nodded.

"You know, I knew a Smith once. He was a blacksmith named James."

"My father's name is James Smith, actually. Finest blacksmith in the Borderlands."

"Your...*father*..." Ruby was quiet, slowly looking up from her stew. She spent a long time studying the Mortal boy's features. Aside from the golden eyes and the slightly pointed ears, the teenager perched in front of her was a dead ringer for his father.

"Mom...?" Moss looked at his mother quizzically. There weren't many times he'd seen that specific look on his mother's face, confusion slowly mixing with astonishment, a sprinkle of nostalgia stirred in for good measure.

Henry studied the Halfling for the first time, really looking over his features. If his nose wasn't quite so defined and his hair wasn't green...he would look an awful lot like...

"Moss, I think..." Ruby laughed at the sheer absurdity of it all. "Well, I think this is your half-brother." She looked between the boys, and it was hard to deny the resemblance.

"Well, I'll be..." Finnigan murmured, his mouth full of bread.

"My dad never mentioned...I didn't know." Henry shook his head. No matter how many times he ran these new thoughts through his head, they wouldn't stick. And yet, the longer he stared at Moss, the more he saw himself in him. "I thought I was an only child."

Moss chuckled softly to himself. Disbelief was an understatement for the things he was feeling. "So did I."

"I loved your father before the Mortal ban." Ruby told Henry. Of all of the things she thought her day would hold, the discovery of what had happened to her dear James was not one of them. She couldn't help but get a little teary-eyed remembering him and all of the feelings she'd felt when he'd been forced to leave her. "All of the Mortals had already been banished from Recensere's Magyklands by the time Moss was born, and I was in no position to seek him out, given the hostility between the Mortals and the rest of the kingdom. And even if I could have, they wouldn't have let him back within the Veil."

"All this time I thought I only wanted an adventure, but...I must have felt that there was more out here for me, that my father was hiding something."

"I'm glad we found you." Moss put a hand on his half-brother's shoulder. "Even if it wasn't in the most pleasant way."

Henry smiled. "So am I."

The conversation continued, with Moss and Henry each filling the other in on their memories from their lives before their adventure had started and their paths had crossed. They found that they had similar laughs, similar smiles. They were alike in more ways than they'd noticed before.

Once the soup was gone, the plate of bread empty, it was with heavy hearts that Henry and the rest of the company prepared to leave. They set out through the mining town, now quiet while the miners stopped to eat a meal before getting back to work.

Despite the new creatures surrounding her, Arya remained unchanged. Well, aside from a new, twisting ache in her head. The noises from the mine must have caused it, she deduced. Deciding not to disclose it to the others, she continued down the paths beside them until they were stopped by a desperate call.

"Hey, wait up!"

"I thought you were staying here!" Arya said, grinning at the Half-Goblin who was sprinting to catch up with them.

Once he finally reached them, Moss stopped for a moment to catch his breath, his hands on his knees. "Well," he exhaled a breath and took another desperate one, "I talked to my mom and we both agreed that this adventure is far from over. As soon as we get you home, I'm coming right back here, but until then, I am at your service, Arya of River's End." He winked at her and then grinned, shrugging. "I've been away for a few years, what's a little while longer?"

"Well, come on then." Agathon urged the group onwards, an amused twinkle in his eyes. Though it was true that the members of this little group hadn't known each other for all that long, he knew that some deep bonds had been forged between them, and none of them were ready to break them just yet. "We haven't got all day."

Chapter 18
The Cavern of Spyrits

The next leg of the journey, out to the Sands of Waye, proved to be longer than any of the group aside from Agathon had anticipated. Arya was unfamiliar with the geography of Recensere to begin with, but even Faiya, Finnigan, and Moss, who had lived within the Veil all their lives, underestimated just how far out east it was.

"Are you alright?" Henry asked softly.

Although the answer was no, Arya nodded. It was a bad habit of hers recently. They'd been walking for a while, making conversation here and there, but Arya had been quiet, her changing eyes locked on the horizon. Her long hair rested on her shoulders, the roots brown and the ends flirting with red and blonde, depending on if Finnigan or Faiya was standing closer to her. She looked like she was in a daze every time Henry glanced over to make sure she was still alive, and not just an empty shell walking beside him.

Agathon took notice of the girl's state too, and examined the sun, which was low enough in the sky to warrant the group setting up camp for the night. He led them a little further, until they reached a place in the woods that was sheltered enough under the tall trees, and then he helped Moss, Finnigan, and Faiya set up while Henry got Arya into a sitting position against a log.

Even when he was right in front of her, Arya still didn't make eye contact with Henry; it was like she was looking right through him. "Arya, are you in there?"

"What?" She shook her head and then looked up at him before nodding and exhaling. "I'm sorry. I'm fine. I think I just need some water."

"Here." Faiya knelt down beside Arya and held a leaf pouch filled with water to the girl's lips. Once she had some liquid in her, she did feel a bit better, but the pinching in her temples was still present and painful.

"Thank you," Arya murmured before zoning out again.

Henry let his gaze linger on her for a little longer before walking over to where Agathon was unpacking food from the additional supplies Kisa had sent him with.

"Hey." Henry stooped down next to Finnigan, who was scraping the muck from his boots with a flat rock he'd found. "Has she been like this?"

"Hmm?" Finnigan hummed, preoccupied before snapping to attention. "Is she okay? Did something happen?"

"She's just...vacant today. It's like she's not even there."

"Arya..." Finnigan's eyes wandered over to her. "She's been getting progressively worse this whole time. Been hidin' it from us, I think. I've never seen her like this, though."

Henry exhaled a sigh, running his hand through his shaggy brown hair. It had been getting longer lately. He figured the condition he was in must be causing his hair all over to grow a little faster. "God, I hope we figure out how to fix her."

Finnigan nodded solemnly. "Me too."

Arya wasn't quite sure how she'd wound up in her sleeping roll, laying against Henry's broad chest, listening to his rumbling snores. The sun was gone, not a hint of it on the horizon, the dark sky filled with stars. If she squinted, Arya could make out Finnigan's form beside her in the sleeping roll next to hers. Faiya was no more than a flickering light tucked into a pillow close to the fire, and Moss' snores, which were nearly identical to Henry's, were the only thing she could pick out that belonged to the Half-Goblin.

She looked around for any sign of Agathon, but she couldn't spot the Centaur, who was certainly taking the first watch of the night. Perhaps he'd wandered off to check the perimeter of their camp.

Figuring that must have been what happened, Arya settled her head back onto Henry's rising and falling chest and closed her eyes, surrendering to the darkness once more.

It was then that she heard the scream.

Looking around frantically, she realized quickly that the scream didn't belong to Henry, Moss, or Finnigan, and it had sounded much too masculine to belong to Faiya. The noise had been loud, and yet, it hadn't stirred any of her companions from their slumber; they were all still fast asleep.

"Henry." Arya gave his chest a pat in an attempt to wake him, but he didn't move. "Henry, did you hear that? I think it was…"

She was interrupted by another horrifying scream. This time, she didn't wait for Henry or any of the others to wake up. Instead, she unfastened the opening of her sleeping roll and stood up, still confused as to how the others hadn't heard it. She didn't even put on her boots before starting to walk towards the source of the noise. There was a white glow in the distance, off in the direction she was heading. Though she tried to avert her eyes from it, they were fixed on the pulsing light, which grew larger the closer she got to it.

For the most part, her trek through the woods was unsettlingly quiet, aside from the snapping of twigs beneath her bare feet and crickets chirping in the dark. She waited for another scream, but it never came. So instead, she followed the wisps of light, waving like flickering white flames, a beacon drawing her closer and closer.

Eventually, the soles of Arya's feet left the leaf-covered forest floors and instead came in contact with cold, solid mud, slick between her toes. She was so focused on the light in front of her that she didn't realize that it was coming from inside of a cave, nor that she was entering it.

She hadn't noticed this little cavern in the daylight due to the long vines hanging in front of it, sunlight bouncing off of the bright green leaves and hiding it from sight. In the dark, it was the light from within it that shined brighter.

Once Arya was a few more steps inside the mouth of the little cave, the light began to move, traveling further down into the stony passage. She followed for a few more steps. The cavern grew dark, the light barely glowing in the distance, fading and fading until Arya was left in total darkness so inky and thick, she couldn't see her own fingers in front of her face. She looked behind her, but instead of the opening of the cave like she expected to find, she was facing a large reflected image of herself, long tangled brown hair resting on her shoulders and dirt smeared down her cheeks.

"*Arya...*" A voice called, and she turned, but she wasn't sure where it had come from. It was a tingle against the back of her neck, a whisper in her soul. The strands of hair sitting in her peripheral vision began to change, but her reflection did not, staring straight at her. This Arya was the Arya of River's End, she realized. It didn't matter where she went or what she became, this Arya would always be the Arya that was inside her.

Glowing white wisps crept up the length of her hair, and her eyes began glowing as well, a bleached white light conquering her irises and pupils. As it happened, her feet left the stone surface of the cavern floor. A cold, weightless feeling struck in the center of her chest and trickled down through her limbs, ice water in her veins.

"You're scared..." The voice echoed deeper into the cave. A shadow was lurking on the rocky walls, but when Arya turned her head to look at it, there was another mirror there instead. This one reflected the Arya that was on the surface at the moment, a floating, ghostly version of her.

"You're a dying star..."

Arya's eyes darted around, determined to find the source of the whispers that were bouncing off of the walls, but everywhere she looked, there was just another mirror, each one reflecting back a different version of herself: the Merfolk with the hair of a Syren and the scream of a Banshee that had pulled Finnigan from the Seaglass Lagoon, the Wynterborn with Fae's fingers who'd saved Henry's life, the High-Elven princess dressed in gold with a rainbow painted across her cheeks, the dark-eyed Spyder who was always ready to attack, and in the center, the Mortal girl with blue eyes that had started it all.

"You're afraid you'll take them down with you..."

"No." Arya's protest came out quietly. She didn't want to believe that. Even if she died, the others...well, most of the others would be okay. Henry, she wasn't so sure about. "I'm...not afraid."

"You are..." the voice disagreed. *"You are a supernova. It will be your fault. It's inevitable."*

"No! Stop it!"

"They've rooted themselves deep in you, and you'll abandon them, leaving them to destroy themselves."

"STOP!"

"You are made of fear, Arya, and your fear is made of you. What **are** *you, Arya Miller? Have you figured it out yet? You have no home. No people. And at the Moons' Cycle's end, You are doomed to —"*

"ARYA!" A deep voice cut through the hushed whispers seeping into her skull, and as soon as the voice bellowed, it shattered the mirrors into fragments of light that fluttered off into the cave like moths made of glass.

Once the ring around her had disintegrated, strong arms enveloped her, and she crashed into a warm chest on her way back down to the floor. Her knees were weak, legs too wobbly to support her, so instead, she found refuge in his arms. It was Henry, but Finnigan was right behind him, concern rooted deep in his green eyes.

"Are you okay?" Henry's large hand tilted Arya's chin up so he could look her over. Once she blinked a few times, her eyes returned to a neutral green instead of the eerie glowing white, and the last of the ethereal wisps flowed out of the ends of her hair.

"I'm okay." She let her delicate fingers wander up and brush against the stubble sprouting from Henry's sharp jawline. Arya quieted his skeptical retort with a soft, "I'm okay *now*."

"What happened?" Finnigan took a few steps closer until he was standing behind where Henry was kneeling, cradling her carefully.

"I...don't know." When Arya looked around at the cave, now filled with mist and sunlight, there were no traces of the haunting that had just occurred there. All that was left was her memory, and at that point, she wasn't so sure she could trust that either.

"The Spyrits." Agathon pulled apart the vines hanging in the cavern's entrance like an earthy curtain, surveying the scene with careful eyes. They weren't in the cave's entrance anymore, but he could still feel their crackling, bone-chilling energy. "They feed on fear. Don't worry too much about whatever they showed you. Just trying to frighten you is all."

Arya nodded, although she knew there was some sliver of truth in the creatures' words.

"Let's get back tae camp, yeah?" Finnigan suggested, jabbing a thumb behind him. "Moss is making breakfast."

Arya hesitated for a long moment before nodding. "Okay."

Henry helped Arya stand, and she took a few wobbly steps until she finally found her footing again. Finnigan took one of her hands with one of his little ones, unsure of how else to support her with his ever-shrinking frame. They both wanted to tell her just how scared they'd been to wake up and find the camp without her, but they reasoned it would only make her feel worse about the whole ordeal.

So instead, they quietly walked with her, the trio trailing behind Agathon. Arya knew the worst of it was over, and yet, she still couldn't help but glance behind her at the cave, its entrance hidden once again, invisible to those who didn't know it was there.

Chapter 19

THE SANDS OF WAYE

After a few days' journey east, the group finally reached the sweltering heats of the Sands of Waye. Just beyond the territory's arid border, they found themselves standing in Coppertown, the relatively new dwelling of a robotic people called the Tynkers.

The Tynkers were known all around as the fixers of the kingdom. They were inventors, doctors, professors, wonderers, some of the smartest people that existed. The Tynkers had once lived in a place called Kettylvale, a beautiful city full of cogs and machines that ran the place for them, but it had been destroyed in the floods that claimed the Ravenglow Forests. And now, the ruins were haunted by a flock of wild Spyrits. Arya was determined to stay as far from that place as possible; one encounter with the ghostly creatures was more than enough for her.

Arya looked around the town's marketplace in awe, admiring all of the moving parts. Metal gleamed in the sunlight, polished so it wouldn't rust in the heat and sand. Gears spun, levers raised and lowered, cranks turned and bands of rubber stretched, each bit and bauble some tiny piece of the greater machine that held the place together.

The people there had grown accustomed to the desert, it seemed, using what appeared to be scraps of canvas to cloak themselves from the rough sand that drifted in the raging winds. They wore large goggles to shield their eyes and the majority of them wore sandals in order to walk on the uneven sands.

And then there was the matter of the Tynkers themselves, who were an amalgamation of many things. They had hair the color of rusty copper and eyes a warm shade of bronze. Pieces of their bodies seemed to be almost Mortal, made of flesh and blood just like the rest of the creatures the group had encountered, and yet, some parts of them, legs, arms, eyes, or even organs, were made of metal machinery, varying from Tynker to Tynker.

Their marketplace's shops were stocked with varieties of goods from the Sands of Waye: fine silken garments with little jingling bits, golden lamps and lanterns of all shapes and sizes, jewelry finer than even Finnigan had seen in all of his days in Clover Town. The Leprechaun shoved his hands as deep into his pockets as he could get them. Stealing from the Tynkers — or giving them any suspicion that he had — was not in his best interest; they'd definitely weld his hand to his face. He flinched at the thought.

As they walked further through the merchants' stalls, Arya felt a new power take control, a foreign Magyk that felt like the sun had soaked into her skin. This far into the Sands of Waye, she was starting to take on the traits of something she'd been convinced didn't exist. She, along with many other people throughout the kingdom, thought these creatures were no more than old Recenserean myths, tales grandmothers would tell their grandchildren at night. Yet even so, her hair rippled with the pink and purple hues known to belong to the Granters of the East, and her eyes brightened until they were as golden as Henry's.

"It's a good color for you," the Mortal boy whispered as he wrapped an arm around Arya's waist and pulled her closer to him. Protectiveness bubbled in his chest as Arya showed yet another side of herself, another reflection of the world around them.

Agathon draped a newly purchased piece of silk over the girl's head, securing it in place over her colorful hair. "It'll draw attention, though," the Centaur warned, wary blue eyes flitting around the marketplace to see if any of the travelers had noticed.

Fortunately, none of them had. Arya's Magyk, as mysterious as it was, remained a secret. For now.

"Granters are in high demand around these parts," Finnigan explained in a whisper, standing on his toes in order to get closer to her ear. "No one's seen one in years. There are rumors they've disappeared forever."

Now, a few days after they had left the Blackrock Mines, he was over a foot shorter than Arya. Finn almost seemed to be getting shorter as they looked at him, his ears pointier, his hair redder, his eyes greener. By sunset, he wouldn't even be at the girl's chest, and the next morning, he'd be even shorter yet.

The Leprechaun was lucky he was quick on his feet, or the Centaur would have strapped him to his back by now so he wouldn't fall behind. Agathon didn't plan to stay in these parts too long. To stay would draw unwanted attention from the dealers that were known to travel through these parts, wanderers from elsewhere that took anything valuable and traded it away for as much money as they could get. People included.

A run-in with them was something they'd like to avoid.

Once the group was properly dressed for the next leg of the journey, Agathon led them on. His hooves weren't much help in the sand, though. They kept sinking into the unstable ground, causing him to stumble.

And for some reason, Arya didn't know how or why, if she focused, she could hear her companions' thoughts. Specifically, their wishes.

This is what was known about the Granters: they could give you your deepest wish with the slightest flick of their wrist, but the Magyk came with a price. However, many people didn't care what the Magyk cost when it could give them anything they dreamed up, which was why Granters were in such high demand.

"Are ye alright there, princess?" Finnigan asked, emptying the sand from one of his buckled shoes, and trading them instead for a pair of sandals. He knew they wouldn't last for long, though; soon, his feet would be even smaller yet, and they'd slip right out of them.

Finnigan wanted to touch the shiny things at the market stalls.

"F-fine," she stuttered, averting her gaze.

Henry took notice of the falter in her tone and looked her over. Her nose was bleeding gold again and her eyes were flickering between gold and silver.

Henry wanted to soothe her.

That wish, she could grant. She slipped into his arms and held on tight. The rest of the group came to a halt. Moss and Faiya and Agathon all looked at her, noticing the stream of golden Magyk that was trickling from her.

Arya's knees buckled and she gripped Henry tightly as her legs gave out, the tall Mortal boy supporting her with ease.

"Henry." Agathon tilted his head, his posture going rigid. Only a few miles into the Sands of Waye, barely beyond the markets of Coppertown, and already they had pursuers.

Henry looked back and spotted the group of men that were clad in black robes, their long swords gleaming in the sun. The dealers had caught a whiff of Arya's Magyk after all. And now, in the face of true danger, his eyes glowed golden. Henry's heart raced, and he felt the changes tearing through every piece of his being.

Moss spotted the first changes happening to his brother and took Arya from Henry's growing arms. The Half-Goblin lifted her up onto Agathon's saddle and then hopped up behind her, holding onto her tight.

Faiya grabbed onto Finnigan and took off, lifting him up and away from the action. He was so small and light that she could carry him without much trouble, and though the process was embarrassing for the shrinking boy, he'd rather be safe in the air than killed by the Wynterbeast.

Agathon broke into a sprint, Arya clinging to Moss and Moss clinging to the racing Centaur. Arya was weak, struggling to get a grip on her location. Her head pounded and the world wouldn't stop spinning no matter how tightly she squeezed her eyes shut.

Moss adjusted his grip, steadying Arya in place as she wavered. Eventually, she slumped back into the Halfling's arms altogether, her body going limp.

Back behind the fleeing group, Henry's frame grew larger. His shoulders became broader and his arms longer and thicker. Fur sprouted up all over his body, and his armor sank into the Magyk that consumed him. He howled at the blue desert sky, sand swirling around him. His eyes locked on the group's pursuers and he lunged, his newly-formed claws emerging from his fingertips.

Moss flinched and turned away from the fight, focusing on the horizon as the Centaur raced further and further, carrying himself and the unconscious girl with them. In the time he'd been with the others, this was the worst of Arya's episodes yet. He had a sinking feeling as to what that meant as far as her current condition was concerned.

Agathon knew this too. He'd been waiting for an episode like this. The Sacreds had been insistent that he bring her to them in the Square if a Magyk flare-up of this kind happened. He was hoping that once they lost their pursuers and managed the beast, he'd have enough time to get her there.

After a while, Agathon stopped running, and Faiya hovered in place, Finn's little legs dangling uselessly in the air beneath them. He listened for signs of the beast, screams or shuffling footsteps, but he couldn't make anything out. In fact, it was *too* quiet. Something was wrong.

Arya stirred from her sleep, awakening in Moss' arms. It took her a few seconds to remember where she was, forcing the twisting pain out of her head so she could focus on the things around her. She was hurting, and they all knew it, but there were more immediate concerns to the group's safety. Like what had happened to Henry, for example. Sure, the beast was occupied for the moment, but as soon as he wasn't...

"Where is he?" Arya's words were no more than a drowsy mumble. "Where's Henry?"

Faiya flew higher, and when he cupped his hands around his eyes, Finnigan was able to look back in the direction they'd come from. There he was, a large, snarling beast, standing over the carnage of the dealers that had been pursuing them. It was not pretty.

"Back that way." Finnigan told her, letting out low whistle. "Holy shamrocks..."

Arya closed her eyes and exhaled a long breath. She had to fix Henry and she knew that, but she didn't know if she would be able to. She had gotten lucky the other time; it had been a spur of the moment sort of thing, an adrenaline rush, a desperate need to heal what she had hurt, but this time...she was afraid. And yet, she didn't have any other choice. She couldn't just let Henry run loose, terrorizing the kingdom. And no matter what shape she was in, she couldn't leave without him.

What kind of friend would she be if she just gave up on him now after everything else they'd been through?

"Take me to him." Arya murmured.

"I don't think that's the best —" Moss started, but Agathon took off at full speed, fulfilling the girl's wishes.

They came upon the mess before they stumbled upon the monster. Blood, thick and red, clumped the sand together. Shreds of black fabric were left clinging to the mangled bodies.

Fresh adrenaline coursed through Arya and she hopped off of Agathon's back, racing faster than he had ever seen a Mortal girl run. She raced through the sand and into Coppertown. All of the shops had been closed up, and all of the people had vanished from sight. They had gone into lockdown, thick metal slabs slammed over all of their windows and doors. These people had been attacked before and they were prepared.

There, in the center of town, sniffing the air for a new feast, blood dripping from his chin, was Henry. Arya could still see the fractured pieces of him in this beastly form. He was in there somewhere. She had to pull him out, or she was sure his new instincts wouldn't hesitate to kill her.

Henry's golden eyes locked onto her, and the huge furry beast took a few steps closer, murder in its eyes. He pounced, and Arya dodged. She reached deep into herself, trying to grasp onto any piece of her Magyk that could help her right now, yet it was something new that wove itself into her.

It was an odd sensation, her arm turning to metal. It felt cold, but not painful. A little uncomfortable and definitely strange, but it didn't hurt. In fact, she hardly felt it. Arya watched as the shiny bronze crept from the tips of her fingers to the edge of her elbow. Gears and cogs surfaced, spinning and rotating in place. From the metal formed a blade, long and sharp, something to defend herself with.

She just hoped that history wouldn't repeat itself. Mortally wounding Henry again was something she'd like to avoid if at all possible.

Before she could do anything to prepare herself, the beast's massive jaw snapped shut around her wrist, but Arya didn't feel anything. The metal that had encased her arm was working as a sort of shield. She tore her arm out of Henry's jaws and stepped away. They were at a sort of stalemate. The metal of Arya's weapon gleamed in the sunlight, and blood dripped from the beast's fangs and claws.

There had to be a way to control this thing inside her, whatever it was, this flux of power that was trying its hardest to kill her. She had done it before, hadn't she?

So, Arya dug as deep as she could, pushing past all of the creatures and foreign Magyk she had picked up along the way and found the resistance piece, still clinging on after all of that time. Her Mortality.

Arya hadn't been completely Mortal since the last time she had lost Henry like this. Maybe it was even before then, before her eyes turned blue, back when she had been Henry's Arya. Not this girl doomed to die in a couple of days. She tapped into that version of herself. Not the healer or the Elven princess or the Syren with a Banshee's voice. Arya Miller, the Girl from River's End. The girl who had a home wherever Henry was, whether it be inside the Veil or out of it.

The pink and purple faded from her hair, the gold left her eyes, and the metal dripped off of her hand as though she was a hot piece of glowing stone. She was left very brunette and Mortal and vulnerable, standing in the wake of this fearsome creature that could lay waste to her at any second.

When he saw his Arya standing there in front of him, the gold in the monster's eyes faltered. It stared at her like she was made of Starlight and then, at long last, the fearsome beast began to shrink.

Agathon and Moss came into the town once they saw that Arya had tamed the beast, followed by Faiya and Finnigan.

Arya had silver blood streaming from one nostril and gold coming from the other, but she stood in front of Henry unafraid of the thing he had become. He had served his purpose. One way or another, he'd gotten rid of the threat to their lives, even if that meant becoming a threat to them himself.

When Henry returned to his usual form, much shorter and smaller than the monster hiding within, he slumped into Arya's arms, ragged, exhausted breaths flowing in and out of him as his body trembled. Arya was shaking too, weak from the ordeal, from the Mortality that was wrapped tight around her being. This part of herself had suppressed the rest for so long, and being it again...hurt more than she remembered.

As her form fluxed from creature to creature, she imagined slipping back into her original form would be like putting on a pair of her shoes back in the village, comfortable and familiar. Instead, it made her feel dizzy, her stomach churning and heart pounding. It was like walking into her house after every piece of furniture had shifted slightly to the left. It was wrong in a way that would take too long to fix.

So as soon as Henry had his bearings, Arya let go. And when she did, a flood of Magyk took control. Her body did not like being Mortal. Not one bit.

Chapter 20

THE MOON CYCLE'S END

Colors flowed through Arya's hair as quickly as water flowing through the stream. Red and blonde and copper curls, pink, blue, green, and mixes of colors even Agathon hadn't seen in his life. Ancient races that had long since been extinct in Recensere, or at least had left the kingdom long ago.

Arya's eyes were doing the same, flashing every color they had learned and then some, every mix of Magyk that had found a place to rest in her soul. Henry took her in his arms as she changed rapidly. The Magyk was taking its toll on her. Her eyes blinked a few times and then snapped shut as her body shook with all of the mysterious forces rushing through her. Henry looked at her with tears in his golden eyes.

This was his fault. Arya had taken on that form to bring him back.

"Boy, get on. *Now*." Agathon ordered Henry. Moss helped him get Arya settled onto the Centaur's back. As soon as they were in place and Arya was secured between the half-brothers, Agathon took off at speeds he had never reached before. Desperation and fear lit a fire beneath him, goading him on, forcing him to sprint faster, faster, faster.

"I thought we were going to the Ring of Fyre next." Henry looked back towards the horizon in the direction of the place where the Dragonfolk dwelled, the tallest volcano in the entire kingdom, and around it, a river of glowing lava. Smoke rose in the distance, a flare that marked where it was to travelers who dared to journey that far east. As fiery as Arya was, he was sure that was a strong contender for the place she belonged. He looked down at his little spitfire, limp in his arms. Her head was resting on his shoulder and her entire body jittered as though she was filled with angry bees.

"We have to get her to the Sacreds as fast as possible. They said to bring her there if she suffered an episode like this. We should have left some time ago, but...the circumstances..." His voice barely even wavered as he ran past the edge of Coppertown, through the grass, and back into the woods. Now that they were out of the sun, the shade gave them solace from the heat, but it didn't help the changing girl any; Arya was still struggling to hold on.

Agathon raced the setting sun, and once it was beneath the horizon, he challenged the moons. As the second in command of the Centaurs, it was his duty to serve the people of the kingdom as a protector of all, appointed by Andreíos, by King Valens and Queen Allora. He had to get this girl to the Square before it was too late.

It took almost the entire night, but finally, they met the path that wove through the areas surrounding the Square, the bustling center of the kingdom, inside which was the castle.

Castle Transverto was a large glimmering thing that shone in the sunlight. It was almost translucent, something that caught the sun in weird ways. And under the moons, as it was now, it seemed to glow. Agathon reached the gate to the city, and at it, there were two Centaur guards in full armor. They recognized Agathon immediately and bowed to him, opening the grand wooden doors to let him and his guests inside the high stone walls of the fortress.

The Centaur's hooves clicked against the stone pathways that covered all of the ground in the Square. The walls here were all brick, sturdy. They would survive an attack, especially one furthered by a group of people who didn't have any Magyk to protect them.

Inside the Square lived a variety of people. There were Starchildren, descendants of the goddess Asteria. There were Vampyres, who lived there studying the Magyk lineage and bloodlines that ran back for centuries. Tynkers built machines to make life there easier, and Witches and Warlocks studied in a college just up the road from where they were. Aside from the college in Terrowin, Recensere's was the most renowned.

Finally, there were the Sacreds, a group of all-knowing elders who overlooked the Square and gave wisdom and insight to the King and Queen and their court.

Agathon came to a stop at the great wooden door of the Sacreds' tall stone tower. There were golden symbols there, a few runes that meant "Wisdom" in Shifterspeak.

Henry hopped down off of Agathon's back first, and Moss helped shift Arya down into the Mortal's waiting arms. He held Arya to his chest, and brushed the changing hair out of her face. It was pink and purple, but didn't stay that way for long. It phased through almost the entire rainbow before Agathon even knocked on the door.

He raised his large fist to rap the brass knocker against the wood, but it swung open first. Henry felt a chill run up his spine. This was too familiar.

The Sacred, who was wearing a long grey cloak tied around his waist with a rope, beckoned them in without saying anything. His eyes were brown, like a Mortal man, and his hair was silver, like the elders' in River's End. The group walked in. Standing around a long slab of stone was a group of Sacreds, all dressed the same as the first. They had vacant expressions on their faces, and their eyes looked hollow, like they had seen things they could never tell.

They motioned for Henry to lay Arya on the stone, and though he hesitated, he did as they asked. He knew questioning them would only waste Arya's very valuable and fleeting time.

Arya was writhing in pain now, eyes squeezed shut and hair changing colors faster than it had before. The changes were coming so quickly that a new color started at her roots before the last had left the ends of her hair. The Sacreds looked to each other and then to the girl. They had foreseen many things, but not this. Not *her*.

As the Magyk coursed through her veins, one of the Sacreds reached out and rested his large hand against the girl's forehead. For a moment, she was calm.

Finnigan tugged on Henry's pantleg, and he let the Leprechaun hop up into his arms. Henry could feel him shrinking, returning to his normal size. He was lucky to be a foot and a half tall, and rapidly losing height. Soon, he was sitting on Henry's shoulder, gripping the boy's collar for stability.

"There was a prophecy about this happening." Spoke the first Sacred, the one that had let them in. "Long ago foretold by the Wizard, Merlin. He told of a girl who had the rainbow in her hair, who would come to us with a great hidden truth."

"Well, she can't tell ye the truth if she's dyin', now can she?" Finnigan raised a tiny fist at the Sacred. Henry shushed him.

"We cannot fix the damage that has been done," spoke another Sacred. This one was older than the first and had the beginnings of a wispy silver beard. "But we may be able to save her."

"I feel a Magyk around her neck. Something that has kept her stable for this long." A third Sacred, this one the youngest in the room, motioned to Arya's collarbones, which were covered up by the flowing silks from the Sands of Waye. Henry's eyes widened in realization.

"It's a...white stone. I found it by the river where we came from." Henry explained as quickly as he could.

One of the Sacreds carefully pulled it out of the fabric of Arya's dress. His eyes widened. "Had she not been wearing this, I fear she would have died as soon as she entered the Veil."

Henry had saved her life. He had unknowingly saved her life.

"The Magyk inside it bonded with her own, meaning she's come into contact with this distinct kind of Magyk before, and that can mean only one thing," the first Sacred told them.

A look of something Henry couldn't describe flooded the Centaur's features. He looked at Arya, his eyebrows furrowing.

How? How could this have happened? How could she be here after all this time?

"Centaur, take her to—" The Sacreds didn't even need to finish their sentence before Agathon helped Henry and Moss get Arya up onto his back. Finnigan was still seated on Henry's shoulder, and Faiya had taken her smaller form and was currently tucked into Moss' pocket, the tension of the situation stealing the voice from her throat.

Agathon raced out the double doors of the Sacreds' tower and through the Square. A few curious onlookers had gathered on the sides of the streets. Many of them had heard about this girl, the one who'd been parading around the kingdom in search of her home.

Agathon charged as if he was racing into war, running faster than he had ever run before. Above them, Recensere's moons were nearing the end of their cycle, inching closer and closer to one another. He had until sunrise, and maybe not even that long, to get her through the front doors of Castle Transverto.

Arya shook, stirring awake in the movement. She looked to Henry, her hair changing from cherry red to sunset orange to as blonde as a summer afternoon. Her eyes were weakly opened, and with a shaking hand, she reached up for his face. Her tears were silver now, and the blood was coming out of her ears in addition to her nose.

"Thank you for coming back for me," she whispered. Henry shushed her, tears forming in his golden eyes. "*Henry…*"

"Shhhh." Henry gently cradled her. "I'm not going anywhere, Arya. I'm right here."

She was slipping and he knew it. It was becoming too hard to keep her eyes open, to force air into and out of her lungs. "It's my turn to leave, I think. Again." Her eyes were fixed on the moons. She blinked slowly a few times and then looked to Finnigan, who was crying in his spot on Henry's shoulder. He was so small. *So* small. "Thank you, Finn. For everything."

"Of course, princess." He sniffled, smiling softly through his tears. "You were my greatest adventure yet."

Agathon raced across the bridge, through the rows and rows of Centaurs standing at attention. Some looked at him as he passed, breaking formation to see who he was carrying, and they were more than shocked to find the changing girl racing towards the castle's gilded gates.

The clocktower in the Tynkers' home chimed as the large brass bells rang. It was almost time.

Just as the last glimmer was leaving the girl's ever-changing eyes, Agathon burst through the castle's front doors and right into the grand hall. All of the castle's guests paused to look at the sudden noise. In had stumbled a Centaur, a Fae, a Leprechaun, a Halfling that appeared to be mostly Goblin, a Mortal boy, and as she straightened up, a possessed look in her eyes and an unearthly straightness in her posture, what appeared to be…

The King stood up from his throne, concern etched deep into his strong features. He had a square jaw covered in stubble. A silver crown adorned with several Shifter Stones, all of them larger than the one around Arya's neck, sat in his white hair, and his silver eyes looked over the girl. He signaled one of the Centaur guards, who then rushed out of the Great Hall and into the Ballroom adjacent to it.

Queen Allora stood beside him, an equally confused and concerned look spread across her fair features. Her long white hair was pulled into an elegant updo that emphasized the graceful silver tiara perched in her locks. Her gown had a bell-shaped skirt that reached the floor, glittering gems stitched into the shiny fabric.

The King and Queen walked down the stairs from the landing where their thrones were situated. Their presence was grand, shiny and silver. It was easy to tell just by looking at them for a single second that these two people were the most important and powerful in all of Recensere.

They studied the girl standing before them as their sons, the princes, walked into the room. They were dressed in outfits almost identical to their father's with crowns that weren't as large as King Valens', but had Shifter Stones embedded into them just the same. They didn't know why their father had sent for them, only that he had done so in the midst of the party that was going on around them.

"This is Arya, your Highness." Agathon bowed before the High King of the land. "A girl from the village of River's End."

"River's End?" the Queen gasped softly, "of the Borderlands?"

"The same." Agathon nodded.

Arya stood in front of the King and Queen. The pain in her head had finally subsided, and as soon as she had noticed the position her friends had taken, kneeling before the royalty of the land, she did the same, dropping to a knee and bowing her head.

"There is no need for that, child." King Valens held out a hand and helped her to her feet. She looked up at him in confusion. There was still sand in her hair and silvery blood caked in it. Her fingernails were grimy and chipped, her face was coated in dirt and sand and her boots had no doubt tracked mud there. But they didn't look at her filth.

Like everyone else in the room, they were focused on *her*.

Arya's hair and eyes had finally stopped flashing colors as her Magyk settled, stabilizing and causing her to take on her natural features. Her hair was white as snow, and her eyes were as silver as Recensere's moons. She looked just like the King and Queen and their sons, the four of whom made up a large fraction of the Shifters that were left after the Rebellion.

"You say you came from the Borderlands, girl?" Prince Valerius, the oldest prince, looked the girl over. She was shorter than him by quite a bit, but he couldn't deny the resemblance to a painting that was hanging in the grand hall, a painting that had been done by a Seer. He had always thought it would be his daughter or granddaughter one day, but no. The painting shared an uncanny resemblance with the girl standing before him.

"I...I did, your Majesty." She spoke quietly, timidly standing in front of the four most powerful people in all of the kingdom, if not in all of Incanto. They were incredible beings, creatures that could take on the form and abilities of any other. "I was raised by Mortals in River's End. They stole me from somewhere in the Magyklands. And I had never known where...until now."

Arya dared to make eye contact with the Queen. Sparkling tears filled the woman's silver eyes. All of those years ago, she had walked into the royal nursery to find a pile of sparkling dust she believed to be her daughter, her only child at the time, the Princess of Recensere. But she wasn't dead; the Mortals had stolen her away, leaving a pile of Shifters' dust in her place to trick anyone that might set out to find her.

The princess they had lost so long ago was standing before them now, a young woman, strong and beautiful. One who had endured so much and had finally come home.

Queen Allora couldn't hold herself back any longer. She rushed to the girl and held her in her arms. King Valens did the same and wrapped his longer, stronger arms around his wife and daughter. The princes stood in confusion, unsure of what was happening.

"People of Recensere," the King announced, turning to face his sons and the rest of the people who were gathered for Prince Valerius' birthday party. "I introduce to you the long-lost heir to the throne of Recensere, Princess Valeria." He then looked down at Arya, a warm and reassuring smile on his face, "My daughter."

To Burn a Book

Johnny and Delphinus stood above the book of Recensere. It had all but consumed Selena. She had been reading it for the past twenty-four hours, so as soon as she took a break to finally sleep, they had taken it, tucked her into Johnny's bed, and driven Johnny's car out into the middle of the woods without telling her.

This was the only way.

That book had become the only thing she thought about, the only thing she *did* aside from sleeping occasionally and eating when she let Johnny feed her. It wasn't good for her. The Magyk was too powerful. Eclypse or not, this thing had to be destroyed before she was too far gone.

Johnny took his lighter out of his pocket and flipped it open, striking a flame. Delphinus had placed the dangerous tome on a tree stump. Johnny held the flame under it, but the fire leaned away, as though being blown by the wind. The closer he held the flame, the farther it reached to get itself away from the book.

This was not going to work.

Delphinus tried to summon a spark of whatever he could conjure to get rid of it, but none of his magic was working either.

Finally, Johnny had an idea. Tucked away in the trunk of his car was a little tank of gasoline, saved for a rainy day or a spontaneous road trip. It was unlikely, but it just might do the trick.

The boys opened the book and splashed the center of it with the foul-smelling chemical, and then Johnny lit it with a burning stick. It ignited with a flash of light and warmth, but the fire went out a few moments later, leaving the pages unburned and plunging the pair into darkness again.

But the book's fight didn't end there.

The words on the page began to glow with silver light and then, there was another flash, this one brighter and longer than the other. When the light dimmed down, Johnny was gone. The book slammed shut. Delphinus walked over tentatively, looking around for his human friend.

"Johnny?" He called, his voice echoing into the cover of the trees. He heard the wings of a bird, startled off. "Johnny?" He called again, louder this time. No answer.

Delphinus lit his palm with magic and used the glowing light to search the ground around him. He felt a presence, but he didn't see Johnny.

And yet, when his magic finally shined down on the weathered cover of the book, he had a sinking feeling inside of him.

Johnny was still there, but he was trapped inside its tattered pages.

THE END

ACKNOWLEDGEMENTS

The first and biggest thank you of this whole process belongs to Jacob Streeter, who spent hours and hours reading *The Lost Queen* and giving me the honest, hard truth when I needed to hear it most of all. You kept me humble and aware of my little fantasy world in ways I never could have been without you. Jacob, you saved this novel with your bare hands. I can't wait to see your name in print someday.

Mom and Dad, as always you were incredibly supportive of me through my whole creative process. Because of you, the two years I've been working on Recensere have flown by. All of the late summer nights I spent rewriting and editing on the couch in the corner of the living room have finally paid off. Thank you for not letting me be lonely through all of it.

Thank you, Uncle Steve, for instilling me with a love of *Harry Potter* all of those years ago. Without you, I doubt I'd be a writer at all. You are the person who got me to love the fantasy genre and all of its magical worlds, creatures, and characters. This book only exists because you inspired me. Thank you for taking me to the theater to see *the Deathly Hallows* and thank you for giving me the first four books of the series for Christmas. I owe you so much more than I'll ever be able to repay.

Thank you to all of my friends and readers from Tumblr for your endless love and support. I wouldn't be anywhere without you. Biene, your art makes me smile on my saddest days. You've brought my writing to life in ways I could have never imagined. It is because of you that my characters breathe.

Finally, thank YOU (yes, you!) for picking up *Recensere: The Lost Queen*. Without you, I wouldn't be able to share these people and places that have been bouncing around in my head for the better part of four years. Thank you for giving this book, and therefore *me*, a chance. I hope you'll return when the next book comes out to read the rest of Arya's story because it is far from over. But if not, thank you for taking this journey alongside me. Maybe the real adventure is all the friends we met along the way.

ABOUT THE AUTHOR

Morgan Marie Steele graduated from Grand Valley State University in 2022 with a degree in Film and Video Production. She's a Michigan girl and spends her summers there with her Mom and her Miniature Schnauzer, Maggie.

Her passion is storytelling, and she spends the majority of her free time playing Skyrim, watching movies, and working on her next novel. She also works on short films from time to time, helping her friends tell their stories too.

If you want to know more about Morgan or her books, you can follow her on her social media:

Twitter/Instagram/TikTok: @msteele1212
Facebook: Morgan M. Steele Books
Goodreads: Morgan M. Steele

Support the

Author!

Leave a Review

.